D1247570

The Untouchables

Eliot Ness
with Oscar Fraley

The
Untouchables

Buccaneer Books
Cutchogue, New York

International Standard Book Number: 1-56849-198-0

For ordering information, contact:

Buccaneer Books, Inc.
P.O. Box 168
Cutchogue, N.Y. 11935

(516) 734-5724, Fax (516) 734-7920

FOREWORD

During the fantastic era of alcoholic madness known as Prohibition, lawless elements which previously had specialized in gambling, vice and shakedowns hit the greatest illegal jackpot of all by catering to the nation's thirst.

Alcoholic beverages were forbidden. Ergo: the people demanded them. It was a cotton-mouthed generation which ignored an irritating law by imbibing such commodities as bathtub gin and needled beer.

Mobsters were quick to capitalize on the demand. The result was that, in a battle for "business" during the "dry" years from 1920 through 1933, they fought among themselves in murderous gang wars, shot up public places with arrogant abandon and made a national institution of the "one-way ride."

Eventually, one strong man came to dominate the national criminal scene. He was "Scarface Al" Capone, the Chicago overlord whose power spread over the entire nation. But when he extended his sphere of operations to legitimate enterprises, the long-idle law enforcement agencies were forced finally to take action.

One group, more than any other, broke the strangle hold which Capone and his mob had on Chicago and the nation.

The Untouchables

This was the United States Department of Justice prohibition detail which smashed his alcoholic empire, cut off his almost inconceivable income, ended his ability to pay millions of dollars a year in graft and helped gather the income tax evasion information which finally sent Capone to a federal prison and crumbled his syndicate.

The leader of this dedicated group was Eliot Ness, a handsome six-footer whose hand-picked gangbusters destroyed the myth of Capone's immunity.

Most youngsters dream, at one time or another during their adolescence, of becoming a detective. But from the time in his teens when Ness avidly began to read Sherlock Holmes, he never wavered from his dream. This desire was heightened when his elder sister married F.B.I. ace Alexander Jamie, later to become chief investigator for the racket-fighting Chicago civic group known as the "Secret Six."

The son of a wholesale baker, Ness was raised with loving strictness by his Norwegian-born parents. From them he learned an appreciation of Shakespeare and the opera; to them he attributed his red-cheeked, well-scrubbed look.

An outstanding tennis player while at the University of Chicago, this quiet man with the firm, deep voice majored in commerce and business administration. But since Sherlock Holmes refused to make way in the mind of Eliot Ness for the world of finance, in his spare time and with a feeling of mild guilt for the hours stolen from his studies, Ness took a jujitsu course and with Jamie's aid became an expert shot at the Chicago police pistol range.

The lure of detective work was too strong to be withstood, and when he was graduated from the University of Chicago in 1925 the humdrum of the business world lost out to the prospect of adventure and excitement. Detective assignments weren't being given to eager collegians, however, and Ness had to be content for two years with a post as an investigator for the Retail Credit Company.

There was little action and much pavement-pounding as he checked credit ratings and investigated insurance claims. Yet it was solid training which qualified him finally for a post with the United States Department of Justice, in the Prohibition Bureau.

But Ness soon discovered that he was a "white knight on a broken-down horse." Sherlock Holmes stamped angrily through his outraged brain as young Ness, incredulous at first, finally admitted to himself that all of the men with whom he served were not *sans peur et sans reproche*.

The utter lack of prohibition convictions in a city as "wet" as Chicago spelled only one thing: bribery. His indignation developed into icy anger and an unshakable determination to do something about it. He laid his plans carefully and with the assistance of Jamie, who had by then left the Department of Justice to become chief investigator for the Secret Six, was able to put them into operation.

Only a small, tightly knit group of hand-picked agents, he reasoned, instead of a large, loosely co-ordinated group, could loosen Capone's grip on the law.

This is the story of that group of ten who literally broke the pay-off power of "Scarface Al" Capone; ten who proved themselves beyond bribery or bullets; ten who became known to the underworld as:

"The Untouchables!"

OSCAR FRALEY

7

The Untouchables

CHAPTER 1

Cigar smoke hung in a heavy blue haze over the long polished table. Ash trays piled high betrayed the inner emotions of the little group as it listened to a tall, spare man with a thin, square-jawed face.

They had every right to be tense and at least subconsciously apprehensive, I thought. For they were the "Secret Six," known more formally as the Citizens Committee for the Prevention and Punishment of Crime, a special committee of the Chicago Association of Commerce. And only a closely guarded anonymity assured their continued well-being.

There may have been fear under their outer determination, but they were the hope of a frightened city as it struggled feebly in a web of bombs and bullets, alcohol and assassination. That was Chicago in 1929, a city ruled by the knife, pistol, shotgun, tommygun and "pineapple" of the underworld, a jungle of steel and concrete clutched fast in the fat, diamond-studded hand of a scar-faced killer named Al Capone.

Yet these six men were gambling their lives, unarmed, to accomplish what three thousand police and three hundred prohibition agents had failed miserably to accomplish: the liquidation of a criminal combine which paid off in dollars to the greedy and in death to the too-greedy or incorruptible.

Now they nodded grim affirmation as they listened to the tall man who was putting their determination into words. The speaker was Robert Isham Randolph, chairman of the Secret Six. His voice rasped as he declared:

"Chicago has the most corrupt and degenerate municipal administration that ever cursed a city—a politico-criminal alliance formed between a civil administration and a gun-covered underworld for the exploitation of the citizenry."

His knuckles rapped loudly against the table.

"There is no business, not an industry, in Chicago that is not paying tribute, directly or indirectly, to racketeers and gangsters. I know you gentlemen agree that we must spend any amount of money necessary to put these hoodlums where they belong."

I felt a tremendous admiration for Randolph as the meeting ended.

It was through Jamie, long famous as "an honest cop," that I had gained entree to the meeting. This handsome, light-haired man was my brother-in-law and recently had left the Department of Justice, where I still was an agent, to become chief investigator for the Secret Six as they pressed home an attempt to obtain conspiracy indictments against the mobsters who controlled Chicago.

As we were leaving, we were met by a rather dapper-looking man who beamed his pleasure at seeing Jamie and stopped to shake hands.

"Well, well, Joe Reilly, the legal beagle," Alex grinned. "Joe, I'd like you to meet Eliot Ness, my wife's kid brother. He's with the Department of Justice, in the prohibition division."

The smile faded from Reilly's face, and he shook hands coolly and impersonally.

"Oh," he said shortly. "A prohibition agent, huh?"

There was a world of unspoken criticism and barely concealed disdain behind those few words. As he made a few brief amenities and then turned away, I could feel a fiery flush staining my cheeks. His manner had embarrassed and humiliated me, and I could feel the hot anger bubbling up inside.

"Take it easy, Eliot," Jamie said, steering me toward the door. "Look, you can't hardly blame this outfit for feeling the way it does about prohibition agents."

My words tumbled out heatedly.

"Why pick on me? Do they think we're all rotten and on the take?"

"Look, Eliot, I know you're on the level," Jamie said. "But you'd be amazed at the things we've uncovered since we started our investigation. With us, everybody has to be suspect. Otherwise there would have been more action against the mobs long ago. Let's have a cup of coffee and I'll tell you a few things that'll open your eyes."

When we were seated in an isolated corner of a neighborhood restaurant, Jamie stirred his coffee thoughtfully for a few minutes. I sat quietly, waiting for him to marshal his

13

thoughts. Suddenly his head shot up and he jabbed at me with his spoon.

"Okay, so you got all shook up because we don't think too highly about prohibition men. I'm sorry. But we've been doing a whale of a lot of investigational work and it's almost impossible to believe some of the things we've discovered."

His voice gathered momentum.

"Let's look at it from the prohibition angle alone, not counting the killings and the other rackets. Would you believe that last year the Capone mob is estimated—and it's a pretty low estimate actually—to have had an income of close to one hundred and twenty million dollars?"

I started to answer but Jamie waved me into silence with the spoon.

"Of that amount, according to what we have been able to figure, they took in twenty-five million from dog tracks and other forms of gambling, ten million from dance halls and vice, ten million from other rackets. . . ."

He paused briefly as if to give emphasis to the final figure and added:

"Which means that off of beer and alcohol alone they took in approximately seventy-five million last year."

I remained silent, digesting those figures, as he paused and took a sip of coffee. I knew that the Capone operations were gigantic, but this was the first time I had heard it nailed down in dollars. Jamie's voice snapped me back to attention.

"From what we have learned, Capone's mob alone has at least twenty breweries in operation. Each brewery puts out one hundred barrels of beer a day—at fifty-six bucks a barrel. That comes to one hundred and twelve thousand daily, and they supposedly are working three hundred and sixty-five days a year.

"Through the breweries and their delivery system," he went on, "they handle alcohol in the form of gin, whisky and what have you. According to our information, they don't make this hard stuff themselves. They buy it from the Maffia. In order to market it, they, the Maffia, have to use the distribution lines of the Capone mob. With hard liquor being a much more expensive product, however, it is reasonable to assume that the volume, dollar wise, is equal to the beer sales."

The spoon was jabbing at me again.

"So we figure that the Capone mob's weekly alcoholic sales volume is in excess of one million and five hundred thousand dollars—or that amount I gave you before of seventy-five million a year." Jamie's voice had a cutting edge. "And yet nobody seems to be able to lay a finger on them."

"You know damned well why," I bridled. "They're greasing too many palms. Every time we pull a raid they've been tipped off, probably by somebody right in our own outfit, and the birds have flown. And when we do make a pinch, what happens? I don't have to tell you. The case never comes up in court."

Jamie nodded.

"Small wonder, because here's something else, Eliot. We figure that about one third of the beer and alcohol take, about twenty-five million a year, is being handed out as graft or protection money. That'll buy a lot of help."

"Not from me," I snapped.

"I know that," Jamie grinned. "But you know what they

say about one bad apple in the barrel spoiling the rest."

I kept thinking about the "bad apples" as Jamie lapsed into silence and stared into his coffee cup. What if there weren't so many apples and you could keep your eye on each one? Then if one developed a spot you could take it out of the barrel and the rest wouldn't be spoiled. Another thing, if they were all good apples to begin with you wouldn't—or shouldn't—have any spoilage. Silly, I thought, but a simple solution.

Then it struck me.

Why not apply this same theory in the Prohibition Bureau?

Enthusasm was so evident in my voice that Jamie's head jerked up when I said:

"Alex, I think I've got it!"

"Got what?"

"Wait a second," I said. "Let me think this thing out."

It didn't take much thinking because it was so simple. Jamie listened attentively as I began to outline my plan.

"Look, it stands to reason that they aren't moving this much beer and alcohol in their hip pockets. They have to sell it in bulk, and to take care of the Loop alone, let's say, there must be from five to ten trucks delivering every day in that locality alone. Now these trucks aren't invisible. But nobody seems to notice them. So there are too many rotten apples, right?"

"Apples?" Jamie asked with a puzzled frown.

"Sure," I said. "They're paying a certain number of the police and prohibition agents just to look the other way. Rotten apples! Right?"

"That's right," Jamie agreed. "A lot of rotten apples."

"Okay," I said. "Now let's look at it this way. Suppose the Prohibition Bureau picked a small, select squad. Let's say ten or a dozen men. Every man could be investigated thoroughly and they could be brought in from other cities, if necessary, to insure that they had no hookup with the Chicago mobsters. No rotten apples. Get it?"

Jamie started to speak, interest putting a spark in his brown eyes, but this time I silenced him.

"Now if this squad were given a free hand—and backing when they did make arrests—I'll guarantee it could dry up this town. And when that happens, and the big money stops rolling in to the Capone mob, pretty soon they don't have that twenty-five million dollars a year to be handing out for protection. Then everybody starts to go to work on them, like they were supposed to do in the first place, and you've got them licked."

Jamie was excited now.

"It sounds good, real good. And what's more, I think I can get the Secret Six to back the idea. If they do, it's as good as in the works. I do know that Randolph has been all the way up as high as President Hoover, but nobody seems to be able to decide just where to start. This just might be the answer, and if the Secret Six gets behind the United States Attorney and puts all those influential shoulders to the wheel, we may see some real fireworks around here."

We had another cup of coffee, silent now as we rolled the idea over in our minds, savoring it. For one thing, I didn't like being lumped with crooks and grafters, and the more I thought of the plan the more I liked it. Jamie did, too, it was evident from his buoyant attitude as we left the restaurant.

17

"I'm going to see Randolph right now," he said briskly. And as he waved one big hand in farewell and started up the street, I called after him:

"Just remember, Alex, this was my idea. So be sure I get picked if it goes through."

Jamie grinned back over his shoulder and went off.

The next few weeks were busy ones because the prodding of the Secret Six finally had stirred the Prohibition Bureau to some semblance of industry, with word coming down from Washington that there had better be more results. Yet it seemed that no matter how many arrests were made, the defendants were usually dismissed for "lack of evidence" or else the cases never came to trial.

No matter where I went or what I did during this period of fretful waiting, I couldn't get the idea of an independent flying squad out of my mind. And as one day followed another without any indications that the idea was even being considered, I almost drove Jamie out of his mind. If I didn't see him personally, I harried him on the telephone.

"What's the idea?" I asked him over and over. "Has Randolph said anything to you about it? Did he put it up to the United States District Attorney?"

"Look, Eliot," he would answer, "I don't hear any more than you do. Randolph's not the kind of man you put the squeeze on and we'll just have to wait and see what happens."

So I fretted and fumed. Ordinarily patient and inclined to be on the quiet side, I became touchy and irritable. Several times, as I recalled the general scorn for prohibition agents which was driven home to me so forcefully that afternoon with Jamie in the office of the Secret Six, I almost felt like chucking the whole business.

It was during one of these periods of depression—something new to me—that I returned to my office one afternoon and found an interoffice memo on my desk. The words leaped up at me and for a few minutes I couldn't hardly believe my eyes. My heart began to beat faster as I read it:

"The United States District Attorney would like to see you in his office at 4:00 P.M. today."

I was there half an hour early, waiting impatiently in the anteroom for the hands of the big clock on the wall to read four o'clock. Two girls behind a wooden railing typed busily, ignoring my presence, but as the hands hit four o'clock one of them picked up the telephone and spoke softly into the mouthpiece. Then she came over to the railing and held open a swinging gate.

"Mr. Johnson will see you now," she smiled.

The United States District Attorney was a bantam rooster of a man who was almost lost behind the mound of papers stacked in front of him on a desk as big as a billiard table. He motioned me to a chair at one corner of the desk.

"Have a chair and forgive me for a few more moments, Mr. Ness. I detest people who keep me waiting and I hate to do it to others. But I must rush these papers out right away. Help yourself to a cigar," he added, pointing to a desk humidor, "and make yourself comfortable."

"Thank you," I said. "I don't smoke. And I'm in no hurry, sir."

George Emmerson Q. Johnson plunged back into his paper work and for the next few minutes I had to subdue my impatience as the sharp-witted, Iowa-born attorney read and signed various letters. Meanwhile, I recalled what I knew of this man who had been practicing law in Chicago since the turn of the century and now was in his late fifties. I smiled to myself when I remembered how, when asked what the *Q* in his name stood for, Johnson admitted that it meant nothing but that he simply had adopted it to distinguish himself from all the other George E. Johnsons.

The desk of the former Iowa farm boy, who had been picked to lay the federal lash across the back of Al Capone, was bare except for the papers on which he worked: the humidor, a pen in a silver holder and a flip-over desk calendar which announced in black lettering that the date was September 28, 1929.

Suddenly Johnson sighed deeply, shuffled the papers back into a pile and rang for his secretary. Then, after handing her the letters and waiting for her to go out and close the door behind her, he sat up in his chair and looked over at me.

"Now, young man, let's get to our business."

"Yes, sir," I replied, waiting for him to start the ball rolling. Nor did he waste any time. In his dry, precise voice he said:

"I understand you're the one who came up with this plan for closing down Capone's breweries which has been brought to my attention by Robert Isham Randolph of the so-called 'Secret Six.' The one to which I'm referring, of course, is that in which there would be a small detached squad operating without supervision."

He paused, as if expecting an answer, squinting at me through rimless glasses.

"Yes, sir. I think it's the only way to really close them down. The way it is, they usually get a tip-off in time to escape—and most of the time they have so much advance warning that we don't even find any equipment to confiscate."

Johnson pursed his lips and said abruptly:

"I like it! I like the whole plan! There's just one question in my mind. Can we find enough honest agents? After all, we have almost three hundred agents in this area now and there doesn't seem to be much happening to the Capone mob and its stills and breweries."

Once again, as on that day in the office of the Secret Six, I began to feel that hot flush creeping into my cheeks and the hackles rising on my neck. Johnson watched me narrowly as I snapped:

"I'm sorry, sir, but we have a lot of honest agents. It's just that we've been getting mighty little co-operation and when we do bring somebody in, why some shyster lawyer—sorry, sir—gets them right out again."

The district attorney's face relaxed in a smile.

"Nothing personal, Mr. Ness. I just wanted your reaction now that you've had a bit more time to consider this plan you came up with."

"Well, sir," I told him quickly, "my only reaction is that I hope, if you decide to go through with this plan, that you might be able to get me named as one of the members of the squad."

Johnson shook his head.

"I'm sorry, I can't do that."

I felt as if the floor had dropped out from under me. I felt crushed and I wanted to shout the unfairness of being excluded from helping to carry out a plan which I personally had devised. But Johnson's words brought me up short.

"I'm sorry, I can't do that because the leader of this squad is going to have a free hand—and not even I am going to tell you whom you should choose."

It didn't register for a moment and then, when it did, I could hardly believe my ears. I stared openmouthed at the district attorney and saw him watching me with a wide smile.

"That's right, Mr. Ness, you're going to get the chance to make your own plan work. And it's going to be up to you to pick your own men."

I sat there gaping, my mind in a whirl, and Johnson chuckled as he opened a desk drawer and took out a cardboard folder. I was so stunned I hardly heard his voice as he took several papers from the envelope.

"I have given a great deal of thought to your plan, Mr. Ness, and also to the right man to pull it off. Frankly, I had several men in mind but you were recommended highly to me by the Secret Six and also," he smiled again, "by your brother-in-law Alexander Jamie, for whom I have a very high regard. This, I might add, weighed in your favor but was not the deciding factor. You see, I've had you investigated rather thoroughly."

"Rather thoroughly" was a mild statement, I realized, as Johnson adjusted his spectacles and began to read from the papers in his hands:

"Eliot Ness, twenty-six years old, six feet tall, 180 pounds, single, blue eyes, brown hair, no scars. Top third of class in both high school and the University of Chicago. Co-operative, neat and modest according to instructors. Played tennis."

Johnson, looking up, said: "I'm a golfer, myself," and then began to read from his file again:

"Lives unostentatiously with parents, both born in Norway. Father is a baker, well thought of but loans money to too many people and never gets paid back. Mother was the daughter of a British engineer. Ness dresses quietly, lives modestly and soberly and has $410 in the bank."

Looking up again with a friendly smile which took the sting out of his words, Johnson added, "I like that. Anybody who was taking graft would have more money in the bank than that or would be throwing it around."

Once more he went back to the file.

"Clean habits, even to visiting the dentist regularly. Pays bills promptly and has excellent credit rating. Good record in the Prohibition Bureau. Shows coolness, aggressiveness and fearlessness in raids. Far more than the average number of arrests; doesn't shirk assignments or complain about extra hours.

"And," he went on, looking up from the papers in his hands, "does complain about not enough raids and not enough convictions."

Leaning back in his chair, Johnson fashioned a tent of his fingers and propped them under his chin.

"There's a lot more here, but that covers most of the points which interested me," he said. "It was your plan—and if you want it, it's your job."

By this time I had recovered my composure. I still felt like leaping out of my chair and doing a jig right there in the office of the United States District Attorney, but I kept my voice even as I told him:

"I hardly know what to say, sir. The best I had hoped

for was that I would be able to get a place on the squad. But to run it, well, all I can say is that I'll bust those breweries or bust in the attempt."

"Fine," Johnson beamed, standing up and reaching across the desk to shake hands. "Now let me fill you in on some other details. I conferred last week with President Hoover regarding the underworld situation here in Chicago and ways and means to dispose of Capone and his hoodlums.

"We have decided that there are two methods of attacking this problem. One is to gather the data to convict Capone for income tax evasion. The other is to fight the Capone mob on prohibition law violations, gather conspiracy evidence and also obtain whatever evidence we can to aid the treasury men."

Without pausing for breath, Johnson raced on.

"Frank Wilson [later to become boss of the Secret Service] has been appointed head of the treasury group which will investigate Capone's finances. You are going to run this special prohibition detail of the Justice Department to close down his breweries and stills, dry up his income and force him to the wall so he won't be able to pay the graft which has been his greatest protection."

I couldn't help interrupting:

"That's fine, if for a change we can make the arrests stick and get some legal action against these hoodlums."

Johnson's eyes snapped.

"Young man, you bring them in—and I'll see to it that they stay in."

Checking his outburst with a half-smile, Johnson said softly:

"I know what you have been up against, but things are

24

going to be different in Chicago from here on in if your squad does the work that I think you intend it to do.

"And now," he added, "as to your end of it, I have already arranged for you to have offices in the Transportation Building. You are going to have an absolutely free hand and you will be accountable to no one except me. And remember, Eliot, I will back you every inch of the way."

"What about men and equipment?" I asked.

"I told you, it's your baby," he said. "You pick your own men, although I would suggest, as per your plan originally, that you keep the squad small. The personnel files of the Prohibition Bureau are at your command, but if you can't get ten or a dozen men to satisfy you there, we'll bring in the files from other divisions. You name it and you've got it, whether it's men, cars, trucks, guns or whatever you need."

Johnson leaned back tiredly and ran a hand through his bushy mop of hair. He sounded almost sorry for me when he spoke.

"You're taking on a dangerous job, Eliot. You'd better pick men who can handle themselves well in a scrap. But I guess you know about that even better than I do."

Then he crouched forward in his chair and stabbed at me with a forefinger.

"There's just one thing I'm going to tell you for sure. I want results!"

"So do I," I told him sharply. "I'm sick and tired of hearing how rotten the Prohibition Bureau is. You'll get results."

"I'll be waiting," were his parting words as he walked with me to the door.

I vowed to myself that he wouldn't have to wait very long.

25

CHAPTER 2

Paper work had always bored and irritated me but now, as I prepared to hand-pick my flying squad, it was a fascinating experience to delve into the dossiers of the available prohibition men.

I had very definite ideas on the type of men I wanted. The success of the entire venture was predicated on there being no "bad apples," and yet the men I was determined to get had to have more to recommend them than unquestioned integrity.

Searching the personnel records of various agents, I ticked off the general qualities I desired: single, no older than thirty, both the mental and physical stamina to work long hours and the courage and ability to use fist or gun. Nor would mere "muscle men" do because each had to have special investigative techniques at his command.

I needed a good telephone man, one who could tap a wire with speed and precision. I needed men who were excellent drivers, for much of our success would depend on how expertly they could trail the mob's cars and trucks. Also, I felt, it might be well to have some fresh faces—from other divisions—who were not known to the Chicago mobsters.

Jamie agreed with me on all of this and suggested the names of some men he thought might fill the bill. Washington supplied the personnel data on these agents, and finally I had weeded out all but fifteen from a starting list of more than fifty.

These fifteen I put under the "microscope."

Two of them were married, but because of Jamie's exceptionally high recommendation I still considered them, even against my personal feeling that it was a job too hazardous for any man with marital responsibilities. In the end, however, I crossed them off because of their families.

A third was weeded out when investigation revealed that he was an inveterate horse player. His reputation was beyond reproach. Yet this was the vulnerable type who might become indebted to someone who could pass out "hot tips" on the races. A fourth fell by the wayside because he dressed too well and spent too much money for a man making an agent's salary of twenty-eight hundred dollars a year—the salary my detail would be receiving.

Finally the fifty starters became nine survivors, and I knew that these were the men I wanted. My intensive probing had turned up no Achilles' heel in their make-ups. They fitted my every qualification and, equally important, each had an impressive record of arrests.

Three of them had, in my mind, been "in" from the beginning. I had worked with them and knew them to be my kind of agents. Further investigation proved that I had been right about their character and caliber.

The first of these was Marty Lahart, an Irishman with a perpetual devil-may-care grin, bright blue eyes and black wavy hair. Marty was a genuine sports enthusiast who could, and did, quote batting averages, football scores and fight results by the hour if given a chance. He carried this love of sports over into his everyday living, maintaining physical fitness through handball and jujitsu. We had had many a long mat bout together, and I knew him to be a game and implacable opponent.

Energetic and seemingly tireless, Lahart filled my bill to perfection, even though you could normally expect the unusual to happen when Marty was around. As I waited for him to answer my summons, I thought with a chuckle about two cases we had been on together.

In one we had raided a combination speak-easy and bordello. The patrol wagon we used was an old-fashioned one, built high off the ground, and it was so jammed that when some of the inebriated ladies started doing the Charleston on the way to the station house, the patrol wagon tipped over. Marty had to sit down on the curb, he was laughing so hard.

Another time I had put him in jail.

This transpired when we received information that, Chicago being in the dire straits it was, bootleg liquor could be bought right in the Shakespeare Avenue police station. So Marty volunteered to be "booked" overnight as my "prisoner" pending arraignment the following day before the United States Commissioner, which was our usual procedure with prisoners.

During the night, by waving the proper amount of money,

he was able to purchase two pints of liquor from the jailer. With this evidence we were able to obtain a search warrant the next day—probably the first warrant ever issued to search a police station.

Although we found and confiscated a large amount of liquor, the police captain in charge of the station claimed it was evidence in cases they had handled. We traded back the liquor for the bootlegger who supplied the station, proving once again that there is no honor among thieves.

My train of thought was interrupted when Lahart, as gay and irrepressible as always, entered my new office and took it in with an admiring glance.

"Some setup, Eliot," he approved. "And I assume that calling me here has some connection."

"Right," I replied. "I'm going to bust Al Capone and I'm hoping you'll help me."

Marty let out a whistle and his eyes lit up excitedly as I told him about my assignment and what I planned to do.

"Count me in, chief," Marty enthused, coining the nickname by which he was to refer to me from that day. "It looks like my uncle was right!"

"How's that?" I asked.

"Well," Marty answered, "I don't know whether you know it or not but I used to work in the post office. It like to drove me nuts, wrestling those sacks.

"Well, my uncle is a captain in the Chicago Police Department. He kept after me for a long time to take the civil service examination for special agent in the Prohibition Bureau. He told me to stay the hell out of the Chicago police because too many of them were on the 'take.' But he also said we Laharts were cops at heart. So finally, looking for excitement, I guess, I took the examination."

My answer came quickly.

"Your uncle was right about too many of the Chicago police," I said. "But God help the guy on my detail who takes a bribe."

Marty's voice lost its lightness.

"As I said, the Laharts were all cops at heart—honest ones. You don't have to worry about me."

"I know that, Marty." Then, standing up to shake hands with my first man, I added: "Glad to have you with me."

The second agent I had in mind was Sam Seager, and he appeared shortly after Marty had left.

Sam was a typical magazine-story detective: rawboned, hard faced and dead eyed. He moved like a cat as he lowered his six feet, two inches and two hundred and ten pounds into a chair. I always thought of Seager as a "gray" man, one who invariably wore gray clothing that seemed somehow to blend with his coloring. Perhaps this had something to do with the fact that at one time he had been a guard in the death house at Sing Sing.

Quiet and unemotional, I knew Sam to be absolutely fearless until he got into a hotel bathroom. There he wouldn't think of getting into a bathtub without first cleaning it thoroughly with a carbolic acid solution he unfailingly carried in his suitcase just for that purpose. An active man whose taste in literature ran largely to westerns, Sam had once read a book about microbes and it shook him up worse than pistols, real or imaginary.

Sam listened without interruption as I outlined the reasons behind his order to report to me. When I finished, he sat there quietly for a few moments and then began to speak in his firm, husky voice.

"It makes me feel pretty good, Eliot, that you picked me. You know, when I left Sing Sing and joined the Prohibition Bureau I thought I was getting into a pretty high-class outfit. But some of the things I've seen and heard about our agents turn my stomach worse than a burning."

"You, too?" I interrupted.

His voice was a growl when he answered.

"You're damned right! I'll be glad to help you clean up Capone—and the rest of it."

That made it two, and I was elated as I waited for the third man I had chosen. This was Barney Cloonan, a barrel-chested giant who fitted the popular conception of the typical Irishman with his black hair, ruddy complexion and ready smile. I had known Barney since I came into the bureau and thought of him, along with Lahart and Seager, as one of my stalwarts when it came to physical action.

Barney's wide shoulders looked broader than ever as he wedged himself into a chair and listened to my outline. There was a note of relief in his musical baritone when he finally said:

"Eliot, I'm with you one hundred per cent. In the first place, I can't hardly stand that office trick I'm on right now. I feel like I'm in a cage and a bit of action will do me good."

"There's likely to be more than a 'bit,' Barney."

"That suits me fine," he nodded.

Actually my main worry was not finding men with an itch for action but an inside man who could double in brass as a "pen and pencil detective."

This man would have to track down every clue we could

uncover during our raids, digging out information concerning who had rented the buildings, who had purchased the trucks and supplies we confiscated and a thousand other details. He must have the patience to check and cross-check such details and file and cross-file reports which would prove the basis for indictments and, ultimately, convictions.

Lyle Chapman was my choice and I felt vastly relieved when he accepted the assignment. Chapman, tall and lean, had been an end on the Colgate University football team. He could handle his share of any physical action, I knew, but he also had a taste for good music and the classics, was a whiz at chess, had been an honor student and possessed a gifted mind. In contrast to Lahart, Seager and Cloonan, Chapman told me he was happiest when working on a difficult office problem.

"How did you ever get into this kind of work in the first place," I asked him.

"I once started a thesis on law enforcement," he replied. "The first thing I knew, I couldn't withstand the urge to get on the inside and see a bit more of it. There was a time, Eliot, when I was torn between becoming either a lawyer or a writer. This work seems to satisfy both of those ambitions."

The next to join my growing force was Tom Friel, a wiry, medium-sized man who was tempered as hard as the anthracite in his native Scranton. Extremely bashful around women —a fact which Lahart was to make much of in the months ahead—Friel was a former Pennsylvania State Trooper who now gloried in the anonymity of an ever-present blue serge suit.

His piercing gray eyes watched me unwaveringly as I described the job we were to tackle.

"I don't have to tell you it's a job which really needs doing," I concluded.

"You don't have to sell me on it, Eliot," he said. "Doing this job would give me more satisfaction than you can imagine."

I was well satisfied with Tom Friel and his attitude, and equally gratified when I met the four others I brought in from outside divisions to round out my squad. These were either men who had been recommended to me by Jamie or men with reputations which had spread throughout the various divisions.

One of them, Joe Leeson, was famed throughout the service as a genius with an automobile. Leeson's ability as a driver was almost legendary: behind a wheel, he could "tail" a suspect's car, drop off to avoid suspicion and unerringly pick up the other car again in some intuitive manner which told him which direction his quarry would take.

Drafted from the Detroit division, Leeson was thirty, the oldest of the men I had selected. As such, I had an important question to ask him.

"This is an odd time to be worrying about it, Joe," I said, "but something has been bothering me. I thought maybe you might be able to give me the answer."

"What's on your mind?" he asked.

"Well, I'm only twenty-six and some of the men, yourself included, are somewhat older and have more experience. I just wondered whether they might be inclined to resent taking orders from me."

Leeson's face split in a grin and he folded his big hands.

"If I were you I wouldn't give it a second thought. Frankly, Eliot, I don't think anybody will envy you the headaches you're going to have running this setup. Speaking for myself, you're the boss and I'm satisfied to be in on the whole thing. I'm certain the others will feel the same way."

The next two men I had selected were the agents destined to be my "walking tails." Both Mike King, a drawling Virginian, and Paul Robsky, who had been a telephone expert in New Jersey, were those "average" men you never notice in a crowd. Average, that is, until it came to a showdown where a man needed more than ordinary courage.

"Robsky is a small man but he's packed with guts," Jamie had summed it up, and that, plus his listing as a telephone expert, made him one of my choices. He habitually wore an old hat that almost came down to his eyebrows, making him appear to the ordinary eye "a man with no face."

King was the kind who could sit in a room with half a dozen people and he would be the last one you would notice. Meanwhile, there wasn't a thing said or done which his rapier mind didn't absorb.

It had been part of my initial plan to keep one man "under cover" so that throughout our operations I would have an agent absolutely unknown to the mob. But I abandoned this idea when I almost "mislaid" my ninth and last man, proving to my own embarrassment right at the beginning that I was a long way from being a Sherlock Holmes.

This man was delayed in leaving the Los Angeles division. Wanting to keep him under cover, I had asked him to check into a hotel under an assumed name on his arrival and to contact me by telephone. He confirmed this by telegram and Lahart happened to be with me when the wire arrived.

"Well, this will round out the team," I said to Marty, handing him the wire which was signed "Bill Gardner."

Lahart read it nonchalantly and then his eyes widened.

"You mean we're really getting Bill Gardner?" he asked.

"What's so surprising about that?" I demanded.

"You mean *the* Bill Gardner?" Marty repeated incredulously. "The Bill Gardner who played for the Carlisle Indians?"

From my investigation into the background of all the men I had picked, I knew that Gardner had played football for Carlisle. I didn't know how well, but sports-conscious Marty did.

"I know he played football there, but I don't know any more than that."

"Played football!" Marty mimicked. "Haven't you read *Collier's* this week?"

I admitted that I hadn't, and Lahart almost snorted.

"Play football! I'll say he did. Listen, Knute Rockne picked his all-time All-America team in this week's *Collier's*. And you know what? He picked Gardner as one of his ends. Right along with such guys as Jim Thorpe, George Gipp and Walter Eckersall. Boy, imagine having him with us!"

But I almost "lost" Gardner before I ever saw him.

Several days later Gardner called and advised me he had checked into the Palmer House.

"I'm registered under the name of Henry Schlitz," he said.

Amused at the manner in which he was starting his new beer assignment, I told him to sit tight and not to contact me until I had been to see him.

Knowing that Lahart was on pins and needles to meet one of his sports idols, I took Marty along with me when I went to the Palmer House to meet Gardner.

But when we inquired for him at the desk, my mind played a sly trick on me.

I asked for "Henry Pabst."

There was no such person registered, naturally, and I had visions of Gardner, with instructions not to contact me, waiting stoically in his room until the case was over. But, I reasoned, a six-foot, three-inch Indian couldn't have checked in without being noticed by one of the desk clerks which the Palmer House has on each floor.

So Marty and I took the elevator to the top floor and started working our way down, asking the clerk at each floor if she had seen a "big Indian" check in. We had worked our way down five floors when we were stopped by two house detectives.

"Just what's on your mind, buddy?" one of them asked me.

I told him my problem, after identifying myself, and he looked at me scornfully.

"Come on down to my office," he instructed.

There he told an assistant to obtain the hotel's daily telephone listing of outgoing calls. Then he jotted down my office telephone number and swiftly began to go through the slips.

After a few minutes he looked up contemptuously and grunted:

"Your man is in Room 515 and his name, for your information is Schlitz—not Pabst!"

What a detective I was, I thought sheepishly as we went up to Gardner's room. But I forgot my embarrassment when the powerfully built man opened the door at our knock.

Gardner had the copper coloring of his Indian ancestors,

together with their high cheekbones and hawk nose, and he moved with the light, unmistakable step of the trained athlete.

It was while I was explaining the details of the job that I abandoned the idea of keeping him under cover. In the first place, Gardner wasn't the type who could walk anywhere without attracting attention by his size and appearance. Secondly, I decided that it was essential to gather my men together for an organizational meeting where they could feel a fraternal bond against the dangers and trials ahead.

They were all on hand the next day when, after general introductions were made and acquaintances renewed, I gave them the complete details of how and why our unit was formed. With painstaking thoroughness I reviewed the financial structure of Capone's alcoholic empire, told them frankly of the retaliation they could anticipate and stated once again what we were expected to accomplish.

Then I laid it right in their laps.

"If anybody wants out, now is the time to say so."

There was no hesitation.

"Count me in all the way!" Lahart's voice was loud and clear.

"Me, too!" Seager boomed.

And one by one, as my eyes picked out the others, they indicated their intention of seeing it through.

What hoodlum, I asked myself, would be able to stand up against such specimens as Lahart, Seager, Cloonan or Gardner? Nor could you overlook Friel, smaller but as deadly as a derringer? There were King and Robsky for shadowing and wire taps, and nobody, I knew, would be able to lose

Leeson with loaded truck or gangland getaway car. And waiting to correlate the evidence we gathered was the canny Chapman.

We were ready to go to work on the monumental job of drying up the alcoholic life blood of the Capone mob.

Chapter 3

But my glow of satisfaction over the highly successful organizational meeting was rapidly displaced by apprehension. Doubts raced through my mind as I considered the feasibility of enforcing a law which the majority of honest citizens didn't seem to want.

I felt a chill foreboding for my men as I envisioned the violent reaction we would produce in the criminal octopus hovering over Chicago, its tentacles of terror reaching out all over the nation.

We had undertaken what might be a suicidal mission.

Possibly time has dulled the satanic memory of the ruthless gangster known as "Scarface Al." But in that year of 1929 he was at the height of his career—that of the most powerful criminal of all time.

On the day when we gathered for the organizational meeting in my office in the Transportation Building, he already had killed—or ordered killed—an estimated three hundred men. Wholesale murder was his favorite method of eradicat-

d opposition. It was an alternative of
y on occasions when his attempts at

thought as I sat there drumming on
fingers, he had already cost the lives
well-publicized blood lettings. These
were only the additional slayings, because gang killings of
minor figures in the underworld were so commonplace that
the ordinary "bumping off" drew little attention.

But the Capone mob had been butchering with a callous
flourish in 1929, defiantly heedless of whether the victim
was a person of consequence or an ordinary "hood." Nobody
was too big or too little to feel the Capone wrath, usually
for the last time.

First, I remembered as I sat there trying to see into the
perilous future, there had been the methodical removal of
Bill McSwiggin, the crusading state's attorney for Cook
County. Despite his prominence, he had been getting into
Capone's patent leather hair and was "rubbed out" by gang-
land guns.

Looking back over the year, I recalled the "St. Valentine's
Day Massacre," in which Capone had virtually wiped out
the brains and backbone of the rival George (Bugs) Moran
gang. Capone simply located an isolated garage in which the
Moran gang met secretly. Then his executioners dressed
themselves in police uniforms and strolled into the garage
in broad daylight without drawing a challenge. The seven
Moran men in the garage were lined up neatly against a wall
—and mowed down in a hail of machine gun fire.

Nor was Capone above taking a personal hand in his own
killings when he was infuriated. Certainly his rage and crav-

ing for vengeance would ultimately be leveled against us if we did a conscientious job.

In preparing to move against him, I had made a long and thorough study of this stocky, powerful man with the long scar on his masklike face. It was all there before me on my desk, and now I reviewed it even though I knew every line by heart.

Al Capone was born in Naples, Italy, on January 17, 1899, and his family emigrated to New York when he was a child. He abandoned school in the fourth grade and began to run the streets and frequent the poolrooms of Brooklyn.

A natural bully, large and strong for his age, it was his inherent brutality which earned him the slicing that was to give him his nickname. At sixteen, he was throwing his weight around in a Brooklyn barbershop when a quick-tempered Sicilian barber grabbed a razor and slashed his left cheek.

Thus was born "Scarface Al."

Meanwhile, he had met a small-time racketeer named Johnny Torrio. The swaggering youngster, who regarded Torrio as his idol, running errands and doing odd chores for him, felt abandoned when Torrio went to Chicago on "business" in 1915. As it developed, Torrio was actually the Capone trail blazer.

In those days, Chicago was cut up into various "territories" by sectional mobs which worked without liaison. One of the strongest gang leaders was "Diamond Jim" Colosimo, who specialized in gambling, white slavery and crooked labor unions.

This was the situation when the Eighteenth—or dry law— Amendment went into effect on January 16, 1920. It paved the way for one of the most lawless periods in American history—thirteen years of bloody gangster warfare to control the illicit liquor traffic which lasted until December 5, 1933, when the Twenty-first Amendment, repealing prohibition, was ratified.

"Diamond Jim" Colosimo moved right in on this liquid gold mine.

But it was so much bigger than anything he had ever handled before that he needed a partner. His choice was Johnny Torrio. And when open war started among the bottle barons, with strong-arm men and " triggermen" at a premium, Torrio remembered the tough and robust Capone kid back in Brooklyn, and he sent for him.

Young Al was a pleasant surprise to Torrio. The gleaming scar on his cheek was a fear-inspiring talisman in itself and now, at twenty, Capone was bigger, stronger and tougher than ever.

One of the Colosimo-Torrio "properties" was a brothel in Burnham, Indiana. There young Capone was installed as "bouncer." This brothel was unique among houses of prostitution because it was situated on the state line between Illinois and Indiana, with half of the house in each state and an entrance from each side.

Here, Capone learned that you could always find a method to beat the law. If a raid was conducted from the Illinois side, the occupants moved to the Indiana side of the house. This method worked equally well in reverse. Soon Capone began sneering loudly, even though it was here that he contracted the social disease which in 1947 sent him to his death, a slack-jawed paretic.

But as the mobs moved in on the beer and liquor traffic, the Burnham house was converted into a brewery. Even then Al was displaying his talents for organization and cold-blooded efficiency and was soon put in charge.

His golden opportunity came swiftly.

In May of 1920, "Diamond Jim" Colosimo was mysteriously shot to death in his Chicago cafe, leaving Torrio, whose predominantly Italian mob was engaged in a vicious territorial war with the Irish mobsters of Dion O'Banion, in need of a partner. Al Capone was his choice.

Almost immediately Capone proved that he had genius for organization, a talent for bribery and an obsession against opposition. Another factor in his favor was the attitude of the general public that drinking in the Prohibition Era was a minor violation bordering on a lark.

Prohibition was designed to keep people from drinking, but no law is successful unless the majority of the people are in favor of it. I don't know how the prohibition law was ever passed but that wasn't my concern. What *was* my concern was the fact that an enormous industry had not gone out of existence but instead had been appropriated by racketeers and hoodlums.

Most criminals are very limited in intelligence or they wouldn't be outside the law. But Capone was a man with an extreme sensitivity to the public taste and great cunning as a corruptionist. Bringing all his skills into play, he was able to get more people to work for him—including gangsters, law enforcement officers, political figures and even judges—than any other criminal in history.

Thus, once certain of their "protection" in all quarters,

Torrio and Capone concentrated on building up their illicit beer business through bulk sales. They were able to do this because they could guarantee regular and uninterrupted deliveries of untaxed beer which actually was a good product.

They hired the best brewmasters available. The "wort," or unfermented malt, was shipped by a fleet of trucks to various fermentation stations. From the breweries it was relayed to the consumer through an elaborately planned distribution system.

This was big business. It had to be. Because to permit such a widespread operation the law enforcement officers either had to be abysmally stupid or "on the take"—and I've known no complete idiots in police work in all my years in the business.

Naturally, there was opposition. But it didn't come from the law. It came from rival gangs jealous of the rise of the Torrio-Capone mob.

The bitterest of the early battles were fought out with the O'Banion mob. Capone emerged victorious in November, 1924, when Dion, the Irishman, was riddled by bullets in a florist shop which he ran as a hobby.

In retaliation, five shots were pumped into Torrio early the next year. Although he survived, he wanted to step out. Suddenly, it was the Capone mob.

With the reins completely in his hands, Capone, only twenty-six, began to take gigantic strides forward. Nobody was too big to bribe, threaten or eliminate. "Scarface Al's" malignant power grew rapidly on murder, graft, corruption and the almighty dollar.

It didn't happen overnight. But within four years after

Torrio's "retirement," Capone had Chicago firmly in his grasp.

The O'Banion mob was liquidated. The "Bugs" Moran gang was being chopped to pieces slowly but surely—and not always slowly, as the "St. Valentine's Day Massacre" showed.

Nor was Capone content with controlling the liquor, beer, vice and gambling of Chicago alone. His designs included a nation-wide syndicate with himself at its head, and meanwhile he began encroaching on what had up to now been legitimate businesses.

One of his first targets was the cleaning and dyeing business. Again he worked on the theory of sales, distribution and lack of competition. Figuring, as always, that if he did away with his competitors the sales and distribution would take care of themselves. Capone instituted the plan of bombing his legitimate rivals out of business. The "pineapple," hand grenade of the underworld, spread a path of death and destruction.

But that was Al Capone's first major mistake. Finally, the citizenry of Chicago became alarmed. It was all right when mobsters were merely eliminating themselves but now people realized that the city was no longer safe for the decent citizens. This was what had aroused the Chicago Association of Commerce, which didn't dare to take open action because nobody was certain who was or wasn't in Capone's pocket, to form the Secret Six.

I suppose I had always been something of an idealist, even though the bright, shining dreams of boyhood don't last very long once you start carrying a badge. But when the United States District Attorney adopted my plan, it had given me an opportunity to strike two blows for my principles. I wanted to help get Capone. I also wanted to help nail all the dishonest cops and officials who had sold out to him.

Unquestionably, it was going to be highly dangerous. Yet I felt it was quite natural to jump at the chance.

After all, if you don't like action and excitement, you don't go into police work. And, what the hell, I figured, nobody lives forever!

But now, as I sat in my office and realized suddenly that we were set to challenge the might and ferocity of the most cold-blooded criminal combine of all time, I knew sudden fear.

Because, starting tomorrow, there wouldn't be a day or night until we broke Al Capone when I'd be able to cease worrying about the men I was about to place in constant danger.

Chapter 4

I knew only too well how perilous it was going to be, because a few weeks earlier I had been within inches of a killing knife thrust just as we made a beginning on the Capone case.

The thought sent a cold chill skating up my spine as I walked into the outer office after my new men had gone.

The powerful man with the incongruous thatch of blond hair who was now lifting his huge bulk out of a chair would always be a reminder.

"You ready to go, boss?" he asked in a deep, booming voice.

"Home, James," I replied. "This may be my last good night's sleep in quite some time."

The big man grinned slowly. This was Frank Basile, my driver, an ex-con I had gambled on to go straight. Already he had proved a good man to have at your back—my back, anyhow.

Basile was a solid 220-pounder and only a steel door could

stand up against his fist or foot. That had been one of my considerations when I took him on, but there was also another reason. He was an Italian who didn't look like an Italian. The men we were after, for obvious reasons of concealment, often spoke in Italian or in a Sicilian dialect, and it was Basile, acting as if he did not understand, who would give me the full translation later.

Looking at his bull neck as he guided my big black Cadillac easily through the crowded, bustling streets of downtown Chicago, I recalled how valuable an asset he had been a short time earlier.

Just before I had been given the go-ahead to form my special detail, the Prohibition Bureau had made one attempt to crack down on the numerous still operators in Chicago Heights, once a residential area, about thirty miles outside the South Side. Now it was spotted with saloons, abandoned houses, barns and garages.

Three of us were assigned to the job: myself; Don L. Kooken, a former trapper and an expert shot, and A. M. Nabors, a handsome, slow-talking Georgian.

As an opening wedge, we had seized one of the stills, and as we expected in a town where too many officers were on the "take," we were approached almost immediately by a representative of the Maffia. This was Johnny Giannini, a slim, dark Italian dressed like a polished stiletto and wearing a diamond stickpin about the size of a lump of sugar.

Giannini popped up out of nowhere as we were putting the still operator into our car.

"Listen, you guys," he said out of the side of his mouth. "Why make all this trouble? We'll take good care of you."

We pretended interest, figuring to make a bribery and conspiracy case and bag the whole lot. We quickly let him know we were intensely interested.

"Okay, then," he said harshly. "Meet me in the Cozy Corners Saloon tomorrow night at eight o'clock."

Kooken grinned knowingly at him and winked.

"All right. We'll be there, Johnny."

That's when I remembered Basile, who had done a short stretch and was going straight. I wanted someone who could understand what was being said when we invaded the enemy's territory. Basile was quickly agreeable. He had gotten into trouble in the first place while "looking for kicks" and this was right up his alley: excitement without getting into trouble with the law.

The next night, Basile with us, we drove to Chicago Heights and parked right in front of the Cozy Corners. We walked in as if we owned the place. There was a policeman in uniform standing at the long, old-fashioned mahogany bar drinking straight whisky. He watched us closely in the long mirror behind the bar as we sat down at one of the tables, and then, shrugging us off, went on with his drinking.

Kooken beckoned to the bartender, saying:

"Tell Johnny Giannini we're here."

"Okay. What'll ya have while yer waitin'?"

We had two gin rickeys which tasted like they were made from low-grade kerosene, after which the bartender, feet slapping across the tile floor, led us into a tiny, airless rear room made even smaller by four wooden tables which were its only furniture. At one of them sat Giannini.

"Glad to know you boys," he said around a toothpick.

49

"Glad you're co-operative, too. We've got things pretty well fixed up around here with the cops and the prohibition boys. No use havin' no trouble."

Kooken sat back in his chair. His voice was purposely greedy.

"That's fine, Johnny. But what's in it for us?"

Giannini didn't waste any time. He drew out an expensive gold-bound wallet, and his long manicured fingers plucked out a stack of twenty-dollar bills.

"There's three hundred bucks. Seventy-five bucks each. How's 'at?"

Kooken's voice hardened.

"It all depends on how much we don't have to see."

"Well," Giannini shot back, "we don't have too much cookin' around here right now. This is about what it's worth."

"Okay," Kooken rasped. "We'll take this for now. We'll let you know later how much we think it's worth."

Giannini's eyes narrowed but he didn't say anything as we left.

The money was marked carefully and we turned in a complete report to the United States District Attorney.

The following night we drove openly into Chicago Heights for a detailed tour. No sooner did we get into the area in which the stills were located than there were two cars following us. We tried again the next evening, and once more we were followed by the squad cars of the racketeers, who made a practice of prowling the streets in the Heights for the appearance of strangers.

A change of tactics was in order. So, wearing old clothes, we approached Chicago Heights by a deserted back road the next night. When we neared the area, we hid the car in an isolated spot and filtered in singly until we were able to gather by prearrangement in the seclusion of a pitch-black alley.

That night we located eighteen stills running wide open.

It wasn't difficult. The stench of the fermenting mash could often be detected as much as half a mile away, and all anyone had to do was follow his nose to the source.

Back at the Cozy Corners Saloon the following night, the bartender recognized us immediately and, after a friendly wave, came to the table with four unordered gin rickeys on a battered aluminum tray.

"How's it?" he asked as he served us the drinks.

I put all the arrogance I could into my voice.

"Never mind the conversation. Tell Giannini we want to talk to him."

The bartender blinked and backed off swiftly.

"Right away! Right away!"

He hurried into the rear room and reappeared almost immediately.

"Johnny sez he'll see ya right now."

Giannini was probing his mouth with the inevitable toothpick as we entered the back room.

"What's on your mind?" he asked.

"Listen, Giannini," I growled. "What do you think we are, pikers? We were through this section last night and we located eighteen stills. We think we got more money coming."

His eyes narrowed.

"Well, now, I'd hafta talk to some of the other boys about that."

My mind was on a conspiracy case which, if we got enough

of these hoodlums in a squeeze, might include corrupt police, city officials and even prohibition agents.

"I'll tell you what you do, Johnny," I told him in a more agreeable tone. "Why don't you get the owners of these stills together and we'll sit down and talk this over."

He chewed his toothpick and then nodded.

"Okay. I'll tell ya whatcha do. I'll get around and see 'em and we'll meetcha at eight tomorra night in Pete Scalonas' joint on State Street."

I was delighted at the way he had fallen into the trap but kept my voice level.

"We'll be there."

Giannini sat motionless, watching us with those snakelike eyes as we left. Out front, as we climbed into our car, Nabors observed:

"I see we have our usual escort."

"They've been with us since the minute we came into the Heights," Basile told him as we drove away.

The next night, a few minutes before eight o'clock, we arrived at Pete Scalonas' saloon. Kooken hadn't been able to come but Nabors, Basile and I were there.

Scalonas was waiting at one end of the bar, a massive, flat-faced man who stood at least six feet, four inches. His voice sounded like gravel pouring into a concrete mixer.

"The guys from the Heights 'll be here purty soon. Let's go inta the back room."

Half a dozen hangers-on watched us as we walked the length of the bar and Pete pushed open the door to the back room. We followed him into a carpetless cell dominated by a round poker table, a shaded light hanging down over its center like a hangman's noose. Cracked green shades were drawn all the way down at the windows and my nose flinched at the odor of stale tobacco smoke and unwashed bodies.

Sitting alone in the corner of the room, chair tilted back against the wall and a cigarette dangling from one corner of his mouth, was a swarthy Italian in a gaudy red-striped silk shirt.

His dark brown eyes inspected us as we entered and then he turned to stare vacantly at the wall. Scalonas jerked his head toward the dark-skinned man.

"Don't worry about this monkey. He works for us. 'Sides, he don't know no English nohow."

We didn't have long to wait before Giannini, as dapper as ever, came in with a short, genial-looking man who resembled a typical Italian businessman. Johnny didn't waste any time.

"This is Joe Martino." His head jerked toward the pudgy little man. "He's head of the organization in the Heights."

We shook hands, Martino acknowledging the introduction pleasantly in grammatical English marked by a heavy accent. I looked hard at Giannini.

"Where's the rest of the owners?"

Johnny's eyes bored hard into me.

"This is all that'll be here. Me and Joe and Pete will do the talkin' for 'em. Whatever we decide goes. Now, let's get at it. What we wanna know is how much you guys want to lay off them stills."

We had agreed beforehand that I was to be the "hungry" one, although actually it made no difference as the money was to be marked and turned over to the district attorney as evidence.

My tone was hard and uncompromising.

"Well, it's going to have to be more than seventy-five bucks a man."

"Jesus," Giannini exploded. "You guys must think we're made of money. The cops is gettin' more dough out of this in the long run than we are."

"My heart bleeds for you," I told him. "Your overhead is no concern of mine. Either we get paid off or those stills don't operate. And we won't settle for nickels."

"Wait a second," Giannini said, beckoning for Scalonas and Martino to join him in the far corner of the room. Their voices rose and fell as they argued heatedly in Italian.

Basile leaned toward me to whisper:

"They're arguing about whether to go five hundred a week."

I didn't want them to arrive at an agreement too quickly and end the meeting. So I broke in on their conversation.

"I don't want to be too unreasonable. How many cops are you paying now in the Heights and how much do they get?"

Martino's face broke into a relieved smile.

"Well, we're paying off . . ."

Giannini cut him off with a fierce scowl and an explosive string of staccato Italian. His eyes were murderous as he glared at me.

"Who we pay and what we pay is our business. We'll give you four hundred bucks a week."

I put on the pressure.

"Five hundred."

"If you don't take the money, we can handle this in another way," he answered.

The threat was obvious.

I grinned at him, looking right into those blazing brown eyes.

"Five hundred."

They turned away and talked again in low tones, stopping to listen as their discussion was interrupted by the voice of the Italian in the barber pole silk shirt who had been sitting silently and almost forgotten in the corner just behind us.

Giannini looked over our heads as if in deep thought and I saw Basile's face pale. Leaning forward in an attempt to be casual, he whispered:

"The silk-shirted one just asked Johnny if he should let Eliot have the knife in the back. And that knife is out and not very far from you."

"Okay, I'll take care of this guy," murmured Nabors, who was sitting on my right. With that, he simply leaned back in his chair, and as his right hand slid casually inside the front of his coat he turned gently toward the silk-shirted man behind me.

I let my breath escape slowly in a deep sigh of relief. I knew that good old Nabors had his hand on the blue steel .45 in his shoulder holster. I also knew that if the man with the knife made the slightest motion to use it, he was going to have a very large, unhealthy hole in that fancy red-and-white silk shirt.

Martino, the round little man, blurted out a hasty "No! No!"

Still, despite Martino's hurried words, the situation remained tense and explosive while Giannini silently calculated the odds. But Giannini's cobra eyes had not missed

Nabors' slight movement as he eased back and covered the Maffia killer.

Suddenly, with several negative jerks of the head, he turned to Martino and Scalonas for a few more words, then spun back to face us.

"Okay," he shot at us. "Five hundred bucks it is."

"Now that's what I call being right sensible," I told him, and then, rubbing it in, held out my left hand, palm up. "Which means that you owe us a little matter of two hundred more dollars for this week."

Without a word, but with the muscles jumping in his clenched jaws, he withdrew two crisp hundred-dollar bills from his wallet and flung them on the table in front of me. I gave him that irritating grin again, almost hoping he'd start something.

"Thanks, Johnny. It's a real pleasure to do business with you. Just make sure it keeps coming in steadily."

With that, we turned and walked out. Nabors catfooted last, his hand unconcernedly clasped on the lapel of his coat and his eyes seldom straying from the knife-happy Sicilian in the gaudy silk shirt until the door closed behind us.

There wasn't a word spoken until we slid into the Cadillac and pulled away from Scalonas' saloon.

"Phewee!" I whistled. "That's one I owe you, Frank. If you hadn't overheard that conversation, I hate to think what might have happened."

Basile craned his neck slightly to look back at me in the rear mirror. I could see the laugh wrinkles around his eyes.

"That's okay, boss. Any time."

The Untouchables

A good man, Frank Basile, and now, as he drove me home just a couple of weeks since that meeting in Scalonas' saloon, I felt he'd make a fine nonofficial member of the Eliot Ness clay pigeons.

CHAPTER 5

The sun glittered brilliantly on the windowpanes when we gathered in my office the next morning. Maybe it was the soul-baring brightness of the day but my worries faded as I looked over this trim, fit and eager crew.

They were "ready."

"The first thing we have to do is clean up some unfinished business," I told them. "We have eighteen stills all marked out in Chicago Heights. We're going to knock them off—tonight."

There was a new alertness among them as they heard my words. Lahart, a delighted grin on his face, nudged Friel and sent a stage whisper through the room.

"I knew we were going to die of boredom on this job."

Seager gave him a silencing look, and Marty subsided as I continued.

"This is only a minor skirmish in what figures to be a full-scale war before we're finished. But there are eighteen stills over there which we spent some time uncovering, and I'm not going to let that work go to waste. Also, there is a guy named Johnny Giannini and a hood in a fancy silk shirt that I'd like to see again."

I told them then in detail how Kooken, Nabors and I had located the stills, accepted a "bribe" in order to start gathering conspiracy evidence against everybody and anybody in the Capone mob that we could nail, and that now I had obtained search warrants to put those stills out of business before we did anything else.

Then I hinted at my future plans.

"After we clean this up, we'll start the tough job. That's going to be the closing of every last one of Capone's breweries in the Chicago area.

"We'd never make any headway by simply raiding isolated stills or closing down the saloons," I added. "From the information we have been able to gather there are close to two thousand speak-easies buying beer in the Chicago area alone. There are only ten of us and they'd open new ones just as quickly as we could close them down. What we're going to do is dry up the source of supply.

"They have to be using an enormous quantity of barrels. So, after we knock off the stills tonight, we're going to locate those barrels, follow them back to the breweries—and hop on the hops."

There was approval in the nods which followed my words. Chapman put in a question.

"Eliot, how do you figure that ten of us can knock off eighteen scattered stills without rousing everybody in Chicago Heights and letting some of the cats out of the bag?"

"We can't," I told him. "But we can make damned certain

we get at least ten of them with somebody in attendance. The rest will be catch as catch can. Now, here's how we're going to work it.

"First of all, I've made arrangements through the United States District Attorney to borrow a number of prohibition agents. We will split up and each of you will take four or five of those men along with you as an independent raiding party. Some of you will have to make two raids, and you may not net anybody the second time around. But we'll get the stills—and probably a fat fistful of the mugs who are running them."

I laid it out completely, impressing on them the necessity for secrecy.

"We're going to pick up these prohibition men and nobody is to get to a telephone," I warned. "Just remember, each one of you is in complete charge of his squad—AND MAKE CERTAIN THEY FOLLOW YOUR ORDERS TO THE LETTER!"

It was early evening before we had straightened out the details. We spent hours going over the map of Chicago Heights, so that each one of my men knew his target and how best to approach it. Then we gathered at a garage which was under government contract to inspect the cars we were going to use and waited for the prohibition men.

Darkness was closing in when they began to appear, and standing outside the big double doors I motioned them into the glass-paneled garage office. It was a large room but with all fifty of us assembled, it was jammed.

Walking into a corner of the room I climbed up on a low bench pushed against the wall and faced them. Immediately they quieted.

"Okay, men, let's get at it," I said. "We've got a number of stills staked out. We're going out to knock them off."

Several of them looked startled, and I had to suppress a smile at Lahart's grin as he watched them.

Then each one of my men stepped forward and picked out four or five men for his squad.

"Is it all right if I make a quick trip to the gents' room?" asked an angular fellow with a bobbing Adam's apple.

"Sure," I nodded, "and Marty Lahart will show you where it is."

From the beginning, I wanted them to know that nobody was getting out of our sight, not even for a moment, to give the mob a tip-off that these raids were going to be made.

Within a few minutes we were loading into the cars. Then, just before we started off, I cautioned each of my men again:

"Remember, nine-thirty on the dot. That way we'll hit them simultaneously and maybe the word won't get around before those of you who have two places to hit can make a clean sweep."

They pulled out of the huge garage one by one. Last of all went our car, with Basile at the wheel, Lahart, two of the prohibition men and myself.

My target was the Cozy Corners Saloon. Giannini had sparked my antagonism with his ruthless certainty that all law enforcement officers could be bought. I wanted to make a clean sweep at his spot, and felt more than justified because our investigation had disclosed that the Cozy Corners was the brain center of the Chicago Heights operation as well as the pickup depot for most of the illicit alcohol trade in the entire Middle West.

We had learned that rumrunners from Iowa, southern

Illinois, St. Louis and even Kansas City used the Cozy Corners as their base of supply. They would leave their cars with the bartender to be driven away by members of the Chicago Heights alcohol mob, while they waited at the bar or availed themselves of what the brothels on the second floor had to offer.

By nine-fifteen we were parked on a secluded side road on the outskirts of Chicago Heights, poised to make our strike. As I sat there in the darkness I knew that our other cars were waiting in other sections ready to descend on the locations I had assigned to them. Cradling a sawed-off shotgun across my lap, I leaned down into the glow of the dash light and looked at my watch. My voice rasped slightly in the darkness.

"Okay, Frank, let's move."

As we slid quietly to a stop in front of the Cozy Corners a quick look at my watch confirmed that we were right on schedule. Lahart leaped out of the car as arranged, hooked a finger at one of the prohibition men and disappeared around the corner of the building to enter from the rear. Waving Basile and the other prohibition man to accompany me, I led a charge through the front entrance and into the barroom.

Four men standing at the long mahogany bar raised their hands swiftly when they saw our guns. The same bald-headed bartender with the dirty apron who had waited on us when we went there to see Giannini was swabbing the mahogany. His eyes bulged when I barked:

"Everybody keep his place! This is a federal raid!"

The words were no sooner out than four revolvers hit the floor and four pairs of arms shot into the air. They stood rigid, heads swiveling to the rear as the door from the back room crashed open and Lahart and the prohibition man who had accompanied him burst into the barroom. Marty's face showed his disgust.

"Hell, Giannini isn't back there."

I pointed to the men standing with their backs to the bar and then to the guns on the floor.

"Well, we caught a few fish. Look at the hardware."

Marty's eyes lighted. Tucking his shotgun under one arm, he picked up the revolvers and jammed all four of them into his belt.

In the far corner of the saloon a flight of stairs led to the upper floor. I pointed to them.

"Maybe Giannini's up there. You others hold on here while Marty and I take a look."

We raced up the stairs with a tremendous clatter and emerged into a long narrow hall which ran the length of the building. A series of rooms faced the corridor on one side. From behind the nearest door came the noise of a radio going full blast.

Marty grasped the knob and flung open the door, charging into the room as he barked:

"Hold it. This is a federal raid!"

Looking past him into a gaudily furnished parlor, I saw half a dozen women, all wearing the kimonos of their profession. Four of them sat frozen at a table with cards scattered across its bare top. Another jerked to attention, a magazine tumbling from her lap. The sixth, sitting on a straight-backed chair as she applied bright crimson polish to her nails, didn't even bother to pull her kimona closed. Looking at Lahart, with the four revolvers tucked inside his waistband and his shotgun in firing position, she giggled:

"Look who's here, girls. It's Tom Mix!"

I couldn't help laughing. Marty turned a fiery red and pulled his coat over the revolvers.

"Won't you boys have a chair and talk this thing over?" invited the blonde.

"Sorry, ladies," he gulped, backing hastily toward the door. "Sorry, but we're right busy."

Quickly we checked the other rooms on the floor, the women clustering in the parlor doorway to watch us. But all of the rooms were empty, containing little more than a bed, a dresser and one or two chairs.

As we walked past the women and retreated down the stairs, the blonde, her kimona still open, stood outlined against the dim hall light and called after us jeeringly:

"Hey, Tom Mix, don't forget to come back and see us. And bring your big boy friend with you."

Marty shot me an embarrassed grin as we got back down to the barroom.

"Jeez," he grunted. "Wasn't that awful?"

I felt keenly disappointed that we hadn't picked up Giannini as the owner of the place but later, after closing up the Cozy Corners, the reports that came in to my raid headquarters in the garage were highly satisfying.

Our operation had caught every one of those eighteen stills, together with a total of fifty-two operators.

Nor was I the only one who was satisfied. Sam Seager had a rare smile on his face when he reported in.

"What's with you?" I asked.

"Look at this," he beamed, holding out one huge hand. "Five real fancy ones."

Nested in his hand were five varicolored matchbox covers.

"So?"

His face colored slightly, like a little boy caught playing with dolls.

"Well, it's like this, Eliot," he fumbled. "When I was a guard in the death house at Sing Sing there was this inmate who saved matchbox covers. He was kind of a pitiful little guy who had knocked off his wife for cheatin' on him. Well, I felt sorry for him and did him a couple of favors. So when he went 'out' he left me the collection. I've been saving them ever since."

He put the covers in his coat pocket and his voice resumed its normal briskness.

"I'm friskin' this guy tonight and I came across these. But I didn't just take 'em. I made the guy take two bits for 'em, five cents each. I wouldn't take anything from those bastards for free."

"Okay, Sam," I told him. "I'll keep it in mind and see if I can come up with any new ones for you. Now let's get on with this job."

There was a lot of work to be done. The stills had to be knocked apart and stored as evidence; reports had to be made out—and there was the matter of preparing to have our prisoners arraigned before the United States Commissioner. But to me it came under the classification of old business.

The major part of the Capone operation was beer, not alcohol. Now we were ready for new business—the task of closing down "Scarface Al's" tremendously lucrative breweries.

65

Chapter 6

It was ironic that our first lead came from Colosimo's, the ill-famed den of the late "Diamond Jim" which since 1895 had been the hub of the Chicago underworld.

Our first move was to make an analysis of how we could hurt the Capone mob and its income the most. If our little group was to make a dent where several hundred prohibition agents and thousands of police had failed, a different kind of game had to be played.

An examination of the records of the Prohibition Bureau revealed that prisoners had never been taken inside of a Capone brewery.

Obviously graft had protected these breweries successfully through the years.

I was soon to learn that this was not the only influence making it almost an impossibility to take prisoners. The fact was that the Capone breweries were manned for only about forty minutes during a twenty-four-hour period.

"It's a cinch," I told my men, "that the barrels have to be

used over and over again. So what we have to do is track those barrels from a speak-easy all the way back to the breweries."

Working on this theory, I split my men up into pairs and sent them out to locate a starting point and "tail" the trucks which picked up the used barrels back to the source of supply.

Leeson and Seager were the first pair to have any success.

Excitement put an edge in Leeson's usually calm voice as he reported to me by telephone from a rooming house on the South Side.

"Seager and I started a watch on a load of barrels in back of Colosimo's at about nine o'clock last night. We thought we were wasting our time but about two o'clock this morning a truck drove up and two men loaded the barrels.

"We followed it all over the South Side and it made a number of pick ups at various speak-easies," Leeson continued. "Finally, the truck was loaded and we tailed it to an old factory at Thirty-Eighth and Shields. We were afraid somebody might spot us and they might break off operations, so later on this morning we rented a run-down room right up the street where we can watch it without being seen."

I assumed, of course, that they had located a brewery and could barely conceal my elation.

"Great work, Joe. Give me the address and I'll be right over there and take a look."

Basile drove me to within two blocks of the address Leeson had given me, and I walked the rest of the way to the red brick house with a sign "Rooms to Rent" in the front window. Leeson had managed to get a front room on the second floor. He met me at the door and led me up a flight of carpeted stairs to the dingy room with a faded rug on the floor, a rickety bed and a wicker armchair in which Seager was re-laxing his huge bulk.

"Home is what you make it," Leeson grinned, "and that window makes up for a lot of things."

We gathered behind the grayish shroud that served as a lace curtain and Seager pointed to a dilapidated factory down the street.

"There she is. But there doesn't seem to be much action."

A close inspection wasn't necessary to show that there was no action at all under way. The place looked as empty as a tomb. I winced as I looked around the dingy room, its stained wallpaper in a huge flowered design unrelieved by anything but a pin-up calendar thumb-tacked to one wall. I didn't envy their surroundings.

"I hope you boys will enjoy your little nest. Because you're going to have to stay here until you get a good line on that place up the street."

Seager groaned as he dragged the wicker armchair to the window so that he could keep a steady watch up the street. Leeson thumped the bed, then kicked off his shoes and stretched out wearily.

"Okay, chief. It was a long night, so I'll catch some shut-eye. Sam, you take the first watch and wake me up when you're ready for this downy couch."

Back at my office in the Transportation Building, reports were trickling in from my other teams. All of them had spotted empty barrels by now and were in the process of backtracking them. Then Cloonan and King came bursting in, Cloonan even more effervescent than usual.

"Chief," he bubbled. "Mike and I have dug you up a nice little brewery down at Thirty-eighth and Shields."

My eyebrows shot up.

"Where did you say, Barney?"

"Thirty-eighth and Shields. We tailed a truckload of empty barrels to an old factory down there."

It was the same one spotted by Leeson and Seager. The one they were watching right this minute. But something didn't smell right. For a brewery taking in that many empty barrels, there should be some action around the factory instead of the abandoned appearance we had observed from the rooming house.

Suddenly the scope of the Capone operations began to dawn on me. This was no brewery. It had to be a plant used only for cleaning the barrels. And if we raided the factory we would be tipping our hand for a collection of empty barrels.

Leeson, calling in the next morning after I had sent Cloonan and King on another lead, confirmed my suspicions.

He went on to tell me then that during the previous night's vigil he had counted twenty-five truckloads of barrels being driven into the cleaning plant.

"Seager finally couldn't stand all the sitting and waiting," Leeson said. "He dug up some old clothes and didn't shave, so he'd look like a vagrant trying to steal something if he got caught. Then he went to the back of the plant, climbed on the roof from the roof of an adjoining building and watched through a skylight while about a dozen guys cleaned those barrels."

There was only one thing left to do. They would have to maintain their vigil, I told him, and then follow the cleaned barrels when they were moved along to the brewery.

"You'd better take it slow, following them only a few

blocks a night, so they don't get wise to the fact that you're tailing them," I said.

Leeson agreed and hung up. I cradled the phone in exasperation. The waiting was nagging at my nerves because I was so anxious to start putting a dent in those breweries.

So I was impatiently ripe—for a mistake—when several days later Friel and Robsky burst into my office with beaming faces and announced that they had located a brewery "for sure."

"We've been watching this place on Lumber Street for two days and there's no doubt about its being a brewery," Friel insisted when I cautioned them that it might merely be another barrel-cleaning plant such as Leeson and Seager had discovered.

"But," Robsky amended, "We could tell the way the trucks were weighted down that those barrels were full when they came out."

I didn't want to take Leeson and Seager off their job, and two of my other teams, checking in daily with reports of progress in backtracking the empties, were too close on the scent to be called off. This left only five of us available for an immediate raid: myself, Friel, Robsky, Basile and Lyle Chapman, the man I was holding in reserve for paper work.

Accompanied by Friel and Robsky, I drove casually past the big wooden-front plant they had located. It was one of a row of warehouses, at 2271 Lumber Street, and on the closed wooden double doors was a sign that read "SINGER STORAGE COMPANY."

The trucks rolled in through those doors each night at about ten, Friel and Robsky reported. That would be the time to crash in, arrest the operators and confiscate the brewery.

Armed with our sawed-off shotguns, crowbars and axes, the five of us drove into the neighborhood that night. Friel and Robsky circled the block and approached the warehouse from the back, while Basile drove Chapman and me to within half a block of the warehouse. There we sat quietly in the car, lights out, watching as several trucks rumbled up to the door at ten o'clock, gave three blasts on their horns as an admission signal and pulled inside when the doors swung open.

Just before ten-fifteen, the time at which Friel and Robsky were to strike from the rear and we three were to break in at the front, I opened the car door.

"All right, let's go. Lyle, you take the crowbar and I'll carry this ax."

Turning to Basile, I handed him my sawed-off shotgun.

"You keep us covered just in case someone starts blasting about the time we go to work with these things," I said.

Basile broke into that huge, white-toothed smile; the sawed-off shotgun looked like a toy in his tremendous hands.

"Anybody sticks his nose out will sure need some plastic surgery," he chuckled.

The second my watch hit ten-fifteen I swung the ax against the lock of those big double doors. The wood splintered and Chapman, forcing the crowbar into the slight opening, pried the lock off with a rasping snap. But it wasn't that easy.

Behind the flimsy wooden barrier was a steel door. The ax clanged harshly on the unyielding metal. I was making it sound like a boiler factory instead of a brewery and sweat popped on my forehead as I wondered whether Friel and

Robsky were getting in at the rear and possibly running into more trouble than they could handle.

"Get behind me," I told Basile and Chapman, giving up on the useless hacking.

I took my .38 Colt from the shoulder holster under my left armpit, stood back a pace and fired a shot into the lock. The door still held. Then, as I fired another shot into the lock, it gave and we shouldered through into a vast, well-lighted room with a concrete floor. Huge vats lined one wall and the sour odor of mash filled the air. Two large trucks were half filled with barrels while other barrels stood ready for loading.

But there wasn't a soul in sight. There wasn't even a sound, except for our panting and the hammering at another steel door at the back of the cavernous room. That would be Friel and Robsky trying to batter their way inside. My voice echoed hollowly as I waved Chapman toward the door.

"Let 'em in and let's see what we've got here."

Well, we had located our first brewery. But the birds had flown. It was easy to see how.

A wooden flight of stairs led to a door that opened onto the roof. While we were attacking the wooden double doors at the front, with Friel and Robsky hammering at the rear, the drivers and brewery operators had simply fled to the roof and escaped through another building by a previously planned route. By now they would be far away, bearing the word that finally the law was getting out of Capone's grasp.

Still, I thought, as I climbed down from the empty roof, it wasn't a total loss.

A survey showed that we had confiscated nineteen 1,500-gallon vats, two new trucks and 140 barrels of beer ready to be shipped. Five of the vats were cooling tanks filled with beer ready to be barreled and delivered. The others were filled with mash.

Subsequent investigation set the value of the plant at $75,000 with a capacity of 100 barrels a day.

It was a start—the first dent in the Capone armament. But I wasn't satisfied. We had taken no prisoners. I blamed myself for not taking my whole crew on the raid, covering all escape routes and bagging the whole lot.

From now on, I decided, it would be different. Each raid would be planned with all the care of a football coach getting ready for a big game—and I had to come up with some method of getting through those steel doors more quickly.

Chapter 7

A way to get inside the breweries came to me as I watched the two captured trucks being driven away to our government-contracted garage.

What I needed was a powerful, ten-ton truck with a special steel bumper covering the whole radiator. Then we could crash through the steel doors which I assumed must be standard equipment at the Capone breweries.

The next morning I sketched the bumper I had in mind and discussed the idea with Chapman.

"I want that bumper really strong," I told him. "And I'd prefer a flat-bed truck on which we can carry scaling ladders. From now on we're going to be ready for any emergency."

Chapman nodded and suggested several ways to improve on the construction of the oversized bumper.

I turned the project over to him and waited for Leeson and Seager to report from their cleaning plant vigil at Thirty-Eighth and Shields. I didn't have long to wait, because that same afternoon, dark circles under his eyes, Leeson came into my office and collapsed into a chair.

"I see by the papers you've been pretty busy," he said. "Well, we have, too. I think Sam and I finally have this one about nailed down."

He told me then how they had tailed a load of cleaned barrels from the cleaning plant to a large garage on Cicero Avenue, in Cicero, adjacent to the Western Electric Company. On this move, the barrel truck had a convoy of two gangsters in a souped-up Ford. The hoodlums wore the pearl gray felt hats with the narrow black bands that were the trade-mark of the Capone mobsters.

"There's a field full of tall weeds right across the street from the garage," Leeson related. "Well, we came in from the other side of that vacant lot late yesterday afternoon and kept watch until three o'clock in the morning before anything happened."

At that time, he said, lights went on in the garage, and a truck pulled out with a load of barrels. Apparently word of our first raid had circulated throughout the mob by this time, because the convoy the day before apparently hadn't been aware of anyone tailing it. Obviously this had been going on so long that they had fallen into the habit of paying little attention to their guard duty.

"But when they pulled out of that garage this morning," Leeson explained, "there was a convoy of two Ford coupés loaded with hoods, and they were really on the lookout. Naturally, we had to lay low because those cars scooted around the neighborhood like a couple of rat terriers. From what we could see, this is only a 'cooling off' spot, not a brewery.

"So what do we do now?" he asked after a pause.

"Here's what you do," I told him. "Tonight, find a hiding place near where you saw that truck disappear with the convoy last night and watch its route without being seen. You'll have to follow it step by step, night by night, until you discover where the convoy leaves it and returns to the 'cooling off' garage."

The following night Leeson and Seager resumed their watch and, working on foot, took up from the point at which the barrel truck had disappeared from view. Three days later they were back in my office. Seager's long, hard face bore a grimace.

"How do you like those guys," he growled. "You must have thrown a scare into 'em the other night."

"What's up?" I asked, fearful that they might have been seen.

Leeson laughed at the look on my face, guessing my thoughts.

"Don't worry, they didn't spot us. It's just that after all our work tailing those barrel trucks, they've only been moving them about a block and a half from the garage where they were 'cooled off.' "

The trucks, he said, were being taken on a long, circuitous route to what must be a brewery at 1632 South Cicero Avenue.

"And what do you think?" Leeson grinned. "There's another vacant lot right across the street for our command post."

Feeling certain that this, finally, was the brewery to which the long trail from Colosimo's had led, I pulled Lahart and Gardner off another lead and we put a twenty-four-hour watch on the South Cicero Avenue address from that friendly field.

Within a few days we learned that the only action taking place around the huge warehouse, after the trucks rumbled into its interior in the small hours of the morning, was between four-thirty and five-thirty in the morning.

Crouched in the tall weeds, tin cans and other debris digging into our ribs, knees and elbows, we saw two ten-ton trucks loaded with empty barrels drive in, while from another direction a tremendous tank truck rumbled in at the same time. After about forty minutes, the barrel trucks reappeared, groaning under their liquid loads, and the obviously lightened tank truck sped away into the darkness. Within a few minutes four or five men, as the case might be, would walk from the darkened building to spots where they had parked their cars in various parts of the neighborhood.

Finally, after several days of watching this procedure, I was convinced that here was the brewery we had been seeking and I began to prepare for a raid.

Meanwhile, I had been filing daily reports with the United States District Attorney's office. There was no censure for having by-passed the Prohibition Bureau in that first raid, but it was suggested that I invite the co-operation of Colonel John F. J. Herbert, head of the Chicago prohibition detail, the next time I made a raid.

I called Herbert and told him we were preparing for another raid and that I would like to use one or two of his agents. My primary purpose was to advise the newspapers that we were co-operating with the Prohibition Bureau.

Herbert told me that he could spare only one man, a new

appointee who had never been on a raid. I jotted down his name and address, and we made arrangements to pick him up at three o'clock the following morning.

I got quite a shock when I drove to his home to get him.

He was a mousy little man with thick, horn-rimmed glasses. I learned later that he had been a clerk in a Chicago department store and had obtained his brand-new job as a prohibition agent through political connections.

He obviously got quite a shock, too, when he stepped into the car with us.

We were a rugged-looking crew, I suppose, to a man unaccustomed to violence. The car's ceiling light polished the high olive cheekbones of Gardner, a muscular 240-pounder holding a sawed-off shotgun nonchalantly on his lap. Sitting next to the big Indian was the slate-faced Seager, his 210 pounds always coiled for action. And Chapman's six-foot, one-inch bulk left little room on the front seat between himself and me.

With a meek nod which acknowledged the introductions, the little man slid into the back seat and was almost lost to view between Gardner and Seager.

"Have you got a gun?" I asked him.

"No," he said. "Am I going to need one?"

I fished into the dash pocket and handed a .38 in a shoulder holster back to Seager.

"Show him how to put it on."

Gardner lifted the little man forward with one hand and stripped back his coat with the other. Seager swiftly tied the holster in place and, as if the prohibition man were a doll, they put his coat back on. Once more, he almost disappeared between them.

I had to stifle a chuckle in the darkness as Chapman drove us to a room I had rented on the Chicago East Side. At least one prohibition agent was going to make a raid this morning!

We gathered in the comfortable, old-fashioned front bedroom of a rooming house run by the widow of a one-time Chicago policeman. They'd get no tip-off information from her. Capone's mob had made her a widow.

My whole crew was on hand this time. Counting Basile and the prohibition agent, there were twelve of us. I laid it out for them like a football play, filling them in on the ten-ton flat-bed truck with the special steel bumper which Basile had driven to the rendezvous.

"Frank is going to drive that thing right through the front doors of the brewery after our pigeons are safely inside," I said. "I'm going to be riding in the cab with him and the prohibition agent. Chapman is going to ride on the back and drop off just before we crash the doors, covering the hole we've made after we go in.

"There are going to be four of you in each of the two cars we're taking. Marty," I announced, pointing to Lahart, "will take charge of the squad which includes Gardner, Robsky and Friel. You four will take the ladders off the truck just before we charge that door, and then get up on the roof—because this time I want every rathole covered.

"Sam will take charge of the second car, which includes Leeson, Cloonan and Mike King. And I want you men to hit 'em from the back—and make damned sure nobody gets out that way."

The raid was planned for 5:00 A.M., the time the barrel trucks should be right in the midst of their loading. Seager's detail, storming the back, was ordered to attack on the dot of five. Meanwhile, Lahart and his roof climbers were to meet the truck just a few doors from the brewery at 4:59—leaving them one minute flat to grab their ladders and scale the roof.

"And remember one thing," I cautioned. "Every one of you, whose job is to cover a possible exit, is to hold his position until I personally release you after it's all over."

Not a single prisoner ever had been captured in a raid on a Capone brewery. This time, I thought as I walked down the stairs and out into a crisp, star-filled night, it was going to be different!

South Cicero Avenue, as Basile trundled our truck onto its cobbled surface, was deserted. Nothing moved except our truck and the two cars behind us. The little prohibition man sitting rigidly between Basile and me hadn't spoken a word since we entered the cab. In the glare of a street light I looked at my watch. We were only a block away now; it was 4:58.

Squirming around to look through the back window, I saw Seager's car swing off around the corner and drift out of sight. Sam wouldn't miss, I knew.

Then, a short distance from double doors, Basile coasted to the curb at my signal and Lahart's car halted right behind us. Four figures emerged, and Gardner was a giant shadow against the moon as he swiftly handed down the long extension ladders. Lahart and Robsky sprinted off with one between them while Friel and Gardner carried the other. The ends of the ladders were muffled, and I knew there would be no grating giveaway as the ladders stretched up against the corner of the brewery and my men swung up out of sight.

The second hand swept up toward the top of my watch. My voice as steady as possible, I directed Basile:

"Hit it, Frank!"

The truck lurched forward with gathering momentum, and Basile had it in second gear when he spun the wheel as the closed doors of the brewery rushed toward us.

I sure hope that bumper does the trick—and that those doors aren't stronger than we are, I was thinking just before we hit with a rending crash.

Splintered wood hurtled down on the radiator, while a flying fragment etched a spider-web design in the windshield glass. My right arm braced against the dashboard, I could feel my left elbow clutched in the terrified grip of the little prohibition man beside me.

Then we were through the doors, as they gave way with a thunderous clap—and my heart sank!

This was no brewery! At least it didn't seem to be, at first glance.

But then I realized that what I was looking at was a wooden wall, painted black, about two truck lengths back from the entrance of the building. It had been designed that way to give the illusion of a vacant garage. The brewery had to be behind that false wall. Pointing forward, I barked at Basile:

"Hit it again! Straight on through that wall!"

Frank didn't question me. He threw the truck into low gear, and again there was a grinding crash, only not as loud this time as the black wall collapsed.

It went down in a shower of dust and splinters, as if some giant hand had drawn a curtain aside to disclose a tableau. Five men stood there, frozen. As I leaped from the truck before it even stopped rolling, one of them, a huge, grizzled man, started to reach for the gun in his shoulder holster.

My Colt was in my hand, and as he made his move I triggered a shot over his head. His hand dropped away as I shouted over the hollow echo of the shot:

"Hold it! This is a federal raid!"

A man standing at the back inside one of the three trucks ducked, then made a dash toward the rear. Chapman started after him when there was a smacking sound and a groan. Seconds later, Sam Seager appeared out of the shadows, dragging the man by the collar of his coat.

"Guess he didn't hear us coming in the back, you were making so much noise with that truck," Sam grinned. "So I fetched him one to let him know the rest of the Marines had landed."

The man Sam had collared, nursing an eye that was going to have purplish overtones next day, was shoved into line with the other four. They were searched for weapons but only one was armed.

I was jubilant as I looked them over. We had made quite a haul. The armed man was Frank Conta, Scarface's old assistant. The burly, round-shouldered man standing sullenly next to him was Steve Svoboda, Capone's ace brewer. The other three were truck drivers. For some reason, they were shorthanded this particular night, but we had netted two big ones, at least. Nobody had escaped.

I climbed a rickety stairway, obviously an escape route to the roof, and called in Lahart and his detail from the top.

Back downstairs, I beckoned to the little prohibition man, still standing motionless and white faced beside the truck with which we had crashed through the doors.

"Keep your gun on these birds. And if they move a finger, don't hesitate to let them have it. They're rough and they play for keeps, so you'd better be prepared to do the same thing."

He gulped and moved a few feet closer to the prisoners. Actually, I didn't expect any trouble. They were unarmed and we were all around them as we set about the process of taking inventory and gathering evidence.

This brewery, I soon saw, was capable of turning out one hundred barrels of beer daily, a production quota which we were to discover later was the general rule in the Capone breweries.

Seven 320-gallon vats lined up in the room, which was cooled automatically so that beer fermented at a slow rate. The brewery was laid out so that each day 320 gallons of wort, or unfermented beer, were brought in by glass-lined tank truck. One hundred barrels would be filled with beer that had been fermented and spiked with carbonated gas.

When our inventory was completed, I had the prisoners taken to the United States Marshal's office. The three trucks, all gleaming new, were sent to the government-contract garage to be held with the two we had already captured. We were starting to gather quite a fleet.

Meanwhile, as we began to destroy the brewing equipment, Chapman noted the numbers of each truck and pump. Later, Chapman's diligent digging uncovered the information that one of the trucks seized on this occasion had been purchased with another truck being used as a trade-in. Circumstances finally connected Al Capone with the purchase and helped tremendously as evidence in the conspiracy case which finally led to his complete undoing.

Quite naturally, I was highly pleased with the results of this night's work. For the first time, a raid on a Capone brewery had netted prisoners, two of them very important ones.

After filing my report, even though I was exhausted, I dropped in to thank Colonel Herbert for lending me his prohibition agent. As I walked into his office, he looked up from his desk and inquired:

"What in the world did you do to him?"

I couldn't imagine what the new little agent had reported.

"I didn't do anything to him. Why, what's the matter?"

Herbert shook his head slowly and looked at me like a kid at the circus inspecting the Wild Man from Borneo.

"He came flying in here, dropped this gun and shoulder holster on the desk along with his brand-new badge and told me:

" 'Colonel, if *this* job is anything like *that,* I quit!' "

He did, too.

As it developed, however, the little man had more than sufficient reason to be frightened. For word soon came to us through co-operative police sources that the mob, in a series of emergency meetings where Sicilian tempers flared to the explosive point, was heatedly discussing what should be done about us.

"The way I get it from some of our stoolies," said a police captain with whom I was friendly, "they've talked about rubbing out your outfit in every way possible, with the accent on the slowest methods imaginable. Two things seem to be holding them back: that Capone isn't here and that you're federal men."

"Scarface Al" at this time still had a short stretch to serve on a Philadelphia gun-carrying charge. Had he been on hand, reprisal probably would have been instantaneous. From our information it was obvious that at the moment the mob was like an octopus without eyes and none of the subchieftains wanted to assume the responsibility for issuing a death warrant against agents of Uncle Sam.

It was a tenuous reprieve, at best, and accounted for the lack of violent opposition as we started our campaign. But I knew it was a shaky respite that could last only as long as the shortest Sicilian temper in the mob. We all realized we were sitting on a keg of dynamite with no means of determining the length of the fuse.

CHAPTER 8

The days flew by swiftly, or, more correctly, the nights, since that was when we did most of our work. The challenge of closing down the Capone breweries became almost an obsession with me, a crusade which forced me to ignore my family and friends and push my men to the limits of their endurance.

I had always been close to my parents, with whom I lived, and had discussed this job with them thoroughly before embarking on it.

Mother worried from the beginning as most mothers would. My father, who had been fifty years old when I was born, faced time and its problems unafraid. Patting Mother's shoulder, he soothed her in his easy manner:

"A man needs an education—and then he has to set his own course."

I knew well from where that stemmed. The day he landed from Norway in 1881 there had been a great commotion.

"I knew that something big was going on," he'd smile at

the memory, "but I didn't speak English and nobody around me at the time spoke Norwegian so I didn't know what."

The "what" was the ultimately fatal shooting of President James Garfield.

Dad worked hard and eventually became the owner of a successful wholesale bakery. By the time I came along, he had the leisure to spend with me and, from his quiet lectures separating right from wrong, I knew what a great impression Garfield's assassination had made on him. And it had been Dad who adroitly fostered my desire to attend the University of Chicago, where I obtained my Ph.D.

Then, too, there was Betty Andersen.

I had met her at a fraternity dance, a petite and beautiful brunette. We were attracted to each other immediately and had a great many interests in common. Soon I had become a regular and welcome visitor at her parents' comfortable home in the Jackson Park area, near the South Shore Country Club.

Practically all of our week ends the previous summer had been spent together. We went swimming and boating, played tennis and laughed away the warm, golden days on picnics and various excursions. I had never before been serious about any girl. But Betty's sparkling brown eyes could make me feel warm all over, and when the wind ruffled her shining russet hair it was all I could do to keep my hands from joining in.

Nothing had been settled between us, yet we both accepted a certain unspoken understanding. It was typical of Betty, as I was forced to break one engagement after another, that she understood and accepted my social dereliction gracefully, but with extreme anxiety.

I had told her of the terrific challenge of this new assignment and she was aware of the risks involved.

"Eliot, this job worries me so much I'm half sick," she argued. "Do you have to go through with this thing?"

Every time I saw her she pleaded with me to give it up but I told her it was something I had to see through.

"Just take care of yourself and see that nothing happens to you," she whispered on one of my flying visits just before we had made our first raid. Then she stood on tiptoe and kissed me lightly.

As I walked away, I felt that I could take on the whole Capone mob singlehanded. But even that memory and my constant desire to be with her couldn't lure me away from the magnetic attraction of the job at hand.

We were still watching that barrel-cleaning plant at Thirty-Eighth and Shields, leaving it in operation so that we could trail the syndicate's trucks back to their various breweries.

And now we started to knock them over with headline-catching regularity.

Using the same tactics, we closed down another big brewery at 3136 South Wabash Avenue a few days after the first successful raid. This one masqueraded as "The Old Reliable Trucking Company." We had one detail covering the roof, where two trap doors gave access to outside fire escapes; another battered in from the rear, and Basile, Gardner and I rode the truck in a smashing entrance through the front doors.

This time, however, we were confronted with a new obstacle: there were two sets of steel doors behind the wooden doors leading in from the street, and a series of electric alarm bells had been installed to start an earsplitting din if entry was forced.

With every exit blocked, though, there was no escape for those inside and we netted five more prisoners. I was rudely surprised as I leaped down from the truck, for there stood my old "friend" Svoboda, the brewmaster taken in our previous raid. He had speedily obtained his release in $5000 bail and was back in business.

"You won't get out so quickly this time," I told him.

Yellow teeth showed in his reply:

"That's what you think, cop!"

This was an even more elaborate plant than the previous brewery. The equipment included two electric beer pumps, an air compressor, fourteen 2500-gallon tanks, and five 1800-gallon cooling tanks. There was even an electric blower to force the fumes out through the roof, and every shade was nailed down and protected by wire screening to ward off "snoopers."

As I was looking over the layout, Lahart came over to me with a big grin and motioned me to accompany him.

"Look at what I found if you want to see a new dodge," he said.

In a corner stood a huge barrel of moth balls which they had spread around the doors and windows in an effort to counteract the beer odor.

We destroyed 40,324 gallons of unbarreled beer and 115 barrels which had already been racked. Then we loaded all the easily movable equipment on two more confiscated trucks that were now being added to our ever-growing fleet. There were raised eyebrows when I said that nobody was to be left on guard.

But I had another trick to play.

We pulled away with a great commotion, as if abandoning the brewery, but when we had left the area I gathered six of my men and told them my plan.

"That trap is pretty well baited, with all those huge and very valuable vats we left there," I explained. "What I want you to do is filter back into the area individually, find yourselves some good hiding places and wait to see whether anybody shows up to try and collect that equipment."

It was a long wait, with one man in a front room, another in an areaway and still others scattered around in places well concealed from street and sidewalk. Hour after hour we bided our time throughout the long night.

Then, at eleven o'clock on Sunday morning, four sedans swept into the neighborhood and cruised about for twenty minutes or so, seeing nothing to excite suspicion as we remained carefully hidden. Then each car took up its strategic position so that a car approaching from any direction could be sighted immediately.

When the sentinel cars were posted, another car rolled into South Wabash Avenue and pulled up in front of the brewery. Three men got out, looked quickly around, then darted inside as the car pulled away.

A few minutes later, a five-ton truck appeared and trundled into the brewery.

At that moment I led a dash from my place of concealment and my other men appeared from their hiding places. The sentinel cars began to blast on their horns as soon as we appeared, but we raced into the building and found that the four men had already loaded one of the 2500-gallon tanks on the truck.

They made no effort to escape, raising their hands and standing quietly as we searched them for arms. One of them turned out to be Bert Delaney, another of Capone's master brewers.

My hunch had turned out to be correct: two of Scarface Al's most valued brewers caught in one raid.

By this time, our backtracking on the empty barrels being collected at the various speak-easies had led us to another cleaning plant. And although the mobsters were very much on the alert, we were able to locate even more breweries through the amazing driving genius of Leeson and the footwork of Friel and Mike King.

In quick succession we knocked over a $125,000 brewery in a garage at 1712 North Kilbourn Avenue, on the North Side, and a $100,000 plant at 2024 South State Street.

The first was discovered through an anonymous telephone tip. As it developed, however, it wasn't a Capone brewery after all, but one operated by George (Red) Barker. Six men were taken into custody there, and we captured another truck, 130 barrels of beer, seven 1250-gallon vats of mash and a 1500-gallon cooling vat filled with beer.

From a stoolie tip, I learned that rival gangs were preparing for a war of vengeance because they blamed one another for tip-offs that had led us to their breweries.

Less than a week later, we closed down the brewery on South State Street, this one operated by the Capone gang. Once again, we used our slightly-the-worse-for-wear truck with the steel bumper to crash through the front doors of the two-story brick building. Five more men were taken into custody, together with one five-ton truck, 67 barrels of beer, 85 empty barrels, eleven 1500-gallon vats which were "working," four 1500-gallon coolers and four other 1500-gallon vats.

These raids were quickly followed up by another; here, though, we ran into a new problem.

This brewery occupied the third and fourth floors of a building used by the Joyce Warehouse Company. The brewery used a large freight elevator to get its materials in and its product out—under the name of the "Alcorn Syrup and Products Company."

Leaving a detail to guard the elevator shaft, I led the rest of my crew up the outside fire escape, and while some of them went up to guard the roof, we crashed in through windows on both the third and fourth floors.

Only two men were on the premises, but it was worth while. We confiscated 62,000 gallons of wort, fifty-one barrels ready for shipment, complete icing equipment, five 3000-gallon pressure tanks, fifteen 3000-gallon aging tanks, special ventilating apparatus and a cooperage plant with 150 finished, but empty barrels.

We also discovered another new piece of equipment: an electric branding machine, which stamped the number "23" within a diamond-shaped outline. Subsequent investigation revealed that this was a visible sign by which Capone "muscle men" could tell at a glance whether speak-easies were using the syndicate's beer.

In spreading our operations to take in a beer-distributing plant we had spotted at 222 East Twenty-fifth Street, we used a new stratagem.

This time Lahart and I simply rode into the plant in an empty beer truck which was returning to the plant for another load of deliveries.

"Let's give this idea of mine a try," Lahart had pleaded. "We'll stand here pretending to fix a tire right where the trucks have to slow down to turn into the plant. Then, as it goes by, we'll just jump into the back and ride on in."

It was such a simple idea that I couldn't resist.

The ridiculous part of the whole thing was that it worked so perfectly. We swung over the tail gate and crouched low as the truck tooted its horn and the double doors swung open. We waited until a man closed the doors and returned to a table where another man was sitting. Then, as the two occupants of the truck got out and joined them at the table, Marty and I eased out of the truck, drew our guns and were almost up to the table before one of them noticed us and just sat there with a stupefied expression on his face.

I kept them covered while Marty opened the doors and the rest of our crew walked in to complete what was probably the easiest raid of our career.

It was profitable, too. We confiscated another truck, 300 barrels and 56 cases of beer and destroyed equipment valued at $25,000. We also appropriated the chart which the men at the table had been scanning. It listed 96 speak-easies served by the plant.

Just as we were preparing to leave, another truck drove up and blared its horn—and we obligingly let it in. That made the score two trucks for the day and added a pair of very surprised prisoners to our scoreboard.

But now the rat was cornered and began to show its teeth.

The day after we had raided the distribution plant, I completed the paper work involved and telephoned Betty. Her low, husky voice soothed my ears, and pleasure came through in her quick answer as I said:

"How would you like to have dinner and see a show with a tired but happy gangbuster?"

After talking to her, I went into the outer office where Basile was reading a newspaper. His face wrinkled in a smile as I said:

"Frank, make sure the car is gassed up and then take yourself off home."

"Got a date, huh, boss?"

I nodded and returned to my office as he pulled himself up out of the chair. I heard him go out and then, a few minutes later, he came bursting in. His eyes were narrowed and his jaw jutted out aggressively.

"Boss, it's gone."

"What's gone?" I asked.

"The car. I left it in the usual place and it just ain't there. Somebody must of took it."

I knew that none of my men would have borrowed my car without letting me know. The answer was obvious. Someone, namely a member of the Capone mob, had stolen it.

This was nuisance retaliation, I thought, as I telephoned the police to give them the license number and ask them to see if they could pick it up. What would happen next had me wondering as I told Frank good night, went downstairs and took a taxicab out to Betty's home.

I didn't have long to wait. The next morning Lahart charged into my office, his perpetual grin missing. He didn't waste time on a preamble.

"Some dirty bastard stole my car last night," he growled. "If I get my hands on the son of a bitch he'll wish he'd never learned to drive."

"Marty," I told him, "you have company. Somebody stole my car late yesterday, too."

Quickly he absorbed my thought.

"Well, well, chief, it looks like the boys in the pearl gray hats are setting out to start squaring a few debts. I've already reported my car stolen," he said harshly. "Now, if it's all right with you, I'm going to pick up Seager and I'm not coming back until I find us another brewery to knock over. I'll show those bastards how to really get tough."

But the mob was ready to get tough, too, as I learned later in the day. The information came from a police lieutenant named Frank McCarthy with whom I had gone to high school.

"Just thought you'd like to know that you're the chief topic of conversation in the Capone mob," he told me over the telephone. "And I'd like to add that, personally, I don't envy you."

"I know they've been discussing us," I replied. "What's new?"

McCarthy's voice was serious.

"Well, this time it's big. Whatever they talked about before was small potatoes because this meeting was called by Frank Nitti—and according to one of our most reliable sources, all the top echelon men were on hand."

This brought me up straight in my chair because "Frank, the Enforcer" was the head of Capone's "Department of Justice." I listened tensely as McCarthy told me that according to his information the meeting had been attended by such gang leaders as Ralph Capone, Jake Guzik, Murray (The Horse) Humphries, "Three-fingered Jack" White, Tony

(Mops) Volpe, "Bomber" Belcastro (the "pineapple" expert) and chief trigger-men "Fur" Sammons and Phil D'Andrea.

"The way I get it, they still aren't quite sure what the 'Big Fellow' would want done against a bunch of federal men," McCarthy said. "They had a helluva'n argument over whether you should be rubbed out. Seems as if they're going to try to get word from the 'Big Fellow,' but in the meantime, Eliot, if I was you I'd walk pretty careful. These guys are nobody to monkey with and any one of 'em might get an idea to go it alone."

Thanking him, I cradled the phone slowly. I hadn't expected the mob to take our assault lying down. But when "Scarface Al's" immediate circle began to discuss our future state of health we were skating on very thin ice.

CHAPTER 9

I was still feeling edgy the next morning when Basile came in from the outer office, closed the door softly behind him and came over to stand by my desk.

"We got the car back, boss," he announced. "The police called just before you got here. They found it over on the South Side, all okay, and I went over and picked it up."

"Fine," I told him. "Did you go over it carefully to make sure they didn't plant anything in it?"

The Capone mobsters were past masters at attaching explosives to automobile starters, putting time bombs under the driver's seat or planting phony evidence.

Basile gave me that big-toothed grin.

"You know me, boss. I wasn't born yesterday. I went over that rig from bumper to bumper."

Our big black sedan with its souped-up motor was Frank's pride and joy. Now that he had that off his mind he said, almost as an afterthought:

"Oh, yeah, boss. There's a young guy wants to see you.

And I hope it's okay, but the way things are starting to cook around here I took the liberty of friskin' him."

"That's one of the hazards of calling on us," I complimented him. "Show him in, Frank, and hang around outside."

"You bet."

Basile strode over to the door and beckoned the man into my office. He was resplendent in a natty pin-striped suit, patent leather shoes and a vivid black-and-orange necktie.

"Mr. Ness," he said, holding out a manicured hand, "I'm George Thomas."

I shook the soft hand and looked him over carefully, wondering what could be on his mind. He was a handsome youngster of about twenty-three with blond, wavy hair, a pale complexion and a voice that was a trifle too high pitched for my taste.

Offering him a seat, I watched him arrange his well-creased trousers with great care and then slide a hand quickly to his necktie to make certain the knot was just right. A real dandy, I thought.

"What can I do for you, Mr. Thomas?" I asked.

"Well," he began, talking quickly in that high, clipped voice, "I'd like to join your squad. I think I could be of great help to you and I'm willing to do almost anything at all to prove it to you."

He looked as if a good strong wind would blow him over, and I almost laughed as I compared him to the tremendous bulk of Gardner or even to the wiry toughness of little Mike King. Controlling my amusement, however, I began to question him.

It soon developed that he had absolutely no qualifications

to become an investigator. He admitted that he had never handled a gun "or even had a fist fight."

"Well," I told him, "the only people we employ are those with the proper background in this sort of work. It's a pretty rough business, you know."

I'll say one thing for him. He was persistent.

"Look, Mr. Ness," he protested shrilly, his voice rising, "there's nothing I'd rather do than be a gangbuster just like you are. Sandra, that's my wife, saw a picture of you in the newspaper and she says to me, 'Now there's a real man.' "

I began to get it. This young man was daffy about his wife and apparently found the reciprocity a bit on the thin side.

"So you want to impress your wife, is that it?"

He gave me one of the nervous little laughs with which he punctuated his conversation.

"Well, you might say that," he agreed. "You see, Sandra is really something. Maybe you've seen her in burlesque— Sandra La Flame, a little redhead with the brightest blue eyes you've ever seen and everything that goes with it. Well, I'd like to make some money to give her some of the things she wants and I'd like to impress her and make her think I'm a big man."

I shook my head.

"George, there are easier ways to make money. And, quite frankly, the only kind of a man I could use right now is somebody who could bring me inside information on the Capone mob."

His eyes brightened.

"A sort of real undercover man, huh? Well, let me tell you, Mr. Ness, I'm just the man you want. I know a lot of the guys in the mob, what with being around the burlesque and speak-easy circuit, and I think I could get you a lot of information."

I sat back and thought about it. I did need a man who could hear what was in the wind and maybe a type like George could manage it.

"Just how would you go about getting started on this thing?" I asked him.

Smiling broadly, convinced that he already had the job that would make him a "big man" wtih his little strip-tease queen, Thomas became expansive.

"Nothing to it, Mr. Ness. It just so happens that I've done several favors for a real big judge. I can get a letter from him to Jake Guzik and in that way land some sort of a job with the Capone mob."

I knew that under these circumstances he could succeed, because "Greasy Thumb" Guzik, treasurer of the Capone syndicate, was always willing and anxious to keep his political connections happy.

"All right," I decided. "If you get that letter and can tie up with the gang, I'll have some assignments for you."

Pumping my hand, George Thomas assured me that "everything will be fixed" and then strutted out. His whistle floated back as the door slammed behind him.

But he wasn't whistling the next day when he came into my office late in the afternoon. There was a pinched whiteness around his lips and a look of indecision in his eyes. The only thing that kept him going, I realized, was the image of the red-haired Sandra, queen of the burlesque circuit.

"I got the letter, Mr. Ness," he said. "Then I went to see Mr. Guzik and he sent me to an attorney who handles the affairs of the Capone gang. And you know what this lawyer says. He tells me that they know I'm working for you and that working for the government will never result in anything good as far as I'm concerned; that the government will use me and then throw me out like an old shoe."

I had suspected that we were being watched closely, and here was concrete evidence that the Capone mob knew who went in and out of our office. The "Kid," as we called him, let me know that they also were digging into my background.

"This lawyer told me that they have information that you got your job under false pretenses by lying about your age," he said in an apologetic tone. "He said it would go hard for you on the witness stand."

I could see what they were planning. The mob was putting pressure on this young man so that, while ostensibly working for me, he could be depended on to tell them everything he learned about us. But that could work both ways, I decided. There was a lot of misinformation I would like to pass back to the Capone mob—and here was a ready tool. Yet I wanted to be certain that he could get safely away when the crisis came.

"All right, let's set it up this way," I told him. "As far as they are concerned, you're working for me but will sell me out if the price is right. They'll pay you plenty for information about me and I'll see to it that you know only the things I want them to know."

Beaming at this solution of his problems, financial and marital, he nodded swift agreement.

"There's just one thing," I added. "I don't want your murder on my conscience."

He paled visibly.

"This is going to be an extremely dangerous bit of tightrope walking," I continued. "So if you go through with it, I want you to start saving money in a Postal Savings Bank." He nodded jerkily, like a marionette out of control.

"I'm not kidding," I added. "You're going to have to show me this balance from time to time so that I know you're putting away a bit of 'going-away' money. Because it just may happen that one of these days you'll have to take a quick trip for your health, and I want to be sure you have the necessary funds on hand."

The "Kid" agreed, and I told him to check with me every morning. This was one pipe line which I wanted to keep flowing.

After he left, I called Chapman, my paper man, and filled him in on the deal I had made with Thomas.

"We certainly can use some outside information even though we're beginning to get a pretty clear picture of what we're up against," Lyle told me. "It's quite an organization Capone has built up."

It was, indeed. Our investigation disclosed that everything the Capone gang did was on a large-scale and highly specialized basis.

From the fragmentary reports of our men, Chapman showed me how a cross section of data from our operatives proved that there was a main sales office on the South Side at which a battery of telephones rang constantly, taking orders from speak-easies for beer and liquor. Another office handled distribution. Still another division managed production: it was patently evident that only the best brewmasters in the country could have planned and laid out these breweries.

"What I'd like to do is tap the telephones at the sales office and put an all-round squeeze on them now that we have figured out a good system to get the breweries," I said.

"It's going to be rough," Chapman replied. "Robsky is a good hand at wire tapping, but that building is isolated and I don't see how we can work it."

Chapman looked puzzled when I said:

"In that case, maybe we can make the mountain come to Mohammed."

The sales office of the Capone mob was located in the Liberty Hotel which, I thought, was quite a word for those vultures to be using. And as Chapman and I discussed the impossibility of tapping the telephones there, a plan had popped into my mind.

If I couldn't tap those wires, why not make the mob move to a place where we *could* tap the wires? In their present state of mind, such a stunt was entirely feasible.

The next morning when the "Kid" came in I started the wheels turning.

"Let them know," I told him, "that we are wise to the fact that their sales office is in the Liberty and that we have them under constant observation there."

After he left, I summoned Lahart and Cloonan and told them that I wanted them to watch the Liberty constantly until they got further word from me.

"And remember," I grinned, "I want you to be seen. Every time they look out of a window or come out to get into a car, I want them to see you."

"Will do," quipped Lahart breezily. "They're going to think we're customers, they'll see so much of us."

A few days later, when the "Kid" came in, he told me that the constant surveillance was causing apprehension among the Capone "personnel" at the sales headquarters.

"Here's some good information you can pass along to them," I told him. "Tell them we're making a voluminous report on the comings and goings there and that next week we're going to pull a raid for evidence."

I instructed the "Kid" to report the next morning on the reaction to this information. He appeared first thing in the morning.

"Boy, did that shake 'em up!" he said. "You know what they're going to do? One of the boys let it drop that they're going to move the whole outfit to a garage two blocks away so that they can drive in and out without being noticed."

Casual conversation with the "Kid" developed the exact location of the garage, and after he left I sent for Robsky.

"Paul, I've got an important job for you," I told him.

Quickly I filled him in on my bluff at the Liberty and the necessity of having a wire tap on the sales office's telephones.

"They're moving into a garage a couple of blocks away," I said, giving him the address. "So this afternoon I've arranged for you to be 'working' for the telephone company.

I had contacted George Harrison, a friend of mine who was a telephone company official, and without revealing the location where I wanted to make the wire tap, had explained the importance of borrowing a telephone company truck. Immediately he had placed a fully equipped truck at my disposal.

"He even sent us phone company coveralls and a company cap," I explained to Robsky. "What I want you to do is to go to that garage, tell whoever's there that there has been trouble in the neighborhood lines—and make certain we've got every phone in the place tapped."

It went off exactly as planned. We hired a room near by, and two days later, when the Capone gang drove up the garage ramp to their new sales office on the second floor, they couldn't take or make a call without our hearing every word.

Of course we couldn't raid every delivery. First of all, we were too shorthanded for such expansive operations. Secondly, if we had made a clean sweep immediately after the sales office was moved, they might have suspected that something was afoot.

We concentrated only on the very largest deliveries. One of the men on duty at our wire tap room would alert me, and a squad of my men would swoop down to confiscate the trucks and take the drivers and the delivery into custody.

Meanwhile, we were still raiding breweries with what was, to me, pleasing regularity. Not so pleasing, however, was the entourage of pearl gray hats we attracted wherever we went.

Obviously, they were still debating what should be done with us and taking no action until Capone's release from prison. But this did not prevent them from conducting their own war of nerves, reminding us constantly that we, too, were under surveillance.

It seemed that every time I looked up there was a pearl gray hat nearby: in restaurants, lobbies, on street corners and even in the elevators in our own office building. There was one in particular to whom I took an active dislike, a beefy individual with the broken nose and puffy eyelids of an ex-prize fighter and a perpetual sneer on his face.

Late one afternoon he actually followed me off the elevator at our floor. I started toward my office, waiting until the elevator doors had closed, then spun around and without ceremony pushed him up against the wall. A thorough frisking showed that he was smart. He didn't carry a gun.

"Whats'a'matter, Mac. Ya lookin' for sompin'?" he inquired.

Then, as I backed off, he casually straightened his coat and jabbed nonchalantly at the elevator button. I watched him, restraining myself to keep from working him over, until the doors opened. As they closed behind him, the harsh voice taunted me:

"Well, stick around a while longer, Mac, and y'll git what y'r lookin' for."

There was a prophetic tone to those words. The vultures were waiting—and getting bolder, certain that sooner or later there was going to be a kill.

CHAPTER 10

"Scarface Al," grown weary of the unending gang warfare, had summoned all the rival Chicago mobsters to a conference at Atlantic City in May of 1929. There they had signed a "peace treaty."

En route back to Chicago, Capone was detained in Philadelphia for a few hours between trains and went to a movie. As he emerged he was recognized by two Philadelphia detectives, and when searched he was found to be carrying a pistol. Within sixteen hours he was tried, convicted and sentenced to one year's imprisonment, the heaviest penalty for such an offense under Pennsylvania law. On May 16, 1929, America's most feared gangster went to prison at Holmesburg.

This meant that, until his release on March 17, 1930—his term reduced to ten months for good behavior—"Scarface Al's" orders were carried out in his absence by his brother, Ralph Capone.

We had discovered that Ralph's headquarters were in the

Montmartre Café, a plush speak-easy near the Western Hotel in Cicero. With the increased pressure, I knew that retributive orders against us would probably issue from there, so that a wire tap on the Montmartre would undoubtedly return dividends.

The question was how to get the tap in operation. On such a tremendously busy exchange, selecting just which phone on which to cut in presented as much of a problem as the technical difficulties involved. I decided I had to get someone inside the Montmartre to study the problem first hand; only then could we ascertain how to make the tap.

There were two prime candidates for such a job: Lahart with his easy propensity for making friends and Friel, a trained observer who could operate shrewdly under the cover of Marty's attention-claiming breeziness. I summoned them for a planning conference.

"What I have in mind is for you two to pick up a couple of girls in one of the speaks and move around town hitting the high spots for a few days," I told them.

"This is work?" Marty chuckled.

"Listen," I said. "If they catch on to you, you're liable to wind up on some lonely road with an even bigger hole in your head. So you'll have to watch your step very carefully. Get some snappy clothes and act like a couple of visitors looking for a good time."

"On expense account, naturally," Lahart persisted.

I couldn't help laughing at him. Here he was, ready to walk into a den of rattlesnakes, and he thought it was a big joke.

"Yes, on expense account. Now, after a few days, I'll come

up with a card for the Montmartre. That'll get you in there so that you can find out who runs the place, how well guarded it is and where the telephone is that they use for most of their business."

"Chief," Marty said as he steamed out with the serious-faced Tom in his wake, "a young lady I've noticed over on State Street is about to have one of the best times of her life—but I don't like the one Friel is getting."

I made it known to the "Kid" on one of his periodic visits that Lahart and Friel had resigned and left town. Marty and Tom, meanwhile, had taken pains to drop out of sight and change their appearance.

Several days later, Lahart called.

"You'd never know us, chief," he said. "I dyed my hair, started a waxed mustache—and these new duds are really something. Friel has some real bright glad rags, too, and without his blue serge suit he's almost too embarrassed to go out in public."

I chuckled at the picture he painted.

"Where are you staying and how does it go?"

"Just fine," he said. "We're at the Western Hotel and have been getting rid of as much beer by drinking it as we ever did pouring it down a sewer. The girls think we're real sports, chief."

I told him that I'd mail him the admission card for the Montmartre, which I had obtained through a police lieutenant friend.

"Send it to 'Mort Lane,' " he said. "That's me in this new league I'm playing. And, oh, yes, you might include a bit more expense money. It seems that prices have been going up since beer is getting a little scarce. Blame it on a guy named Eliot Ness."

I told him I'd send the money, and then Lahart really astounded me. His voice became serious as he said:

"Do me a favor, Eliot. Tell Seager I've picked up a swell bunch of matchbox covers for his collection. He'll be real pleased."

Then Marty's voice was bubbling again just before he hung up.

"I told you, chief. I don't like the one Friel got!" he repeated.

Putting some money and the admission card to the Montmartre into an envelope, I mailed them to "Mort Lane" at the Western Hotel and sat back to await developments.

They weren't long in coming. The telephone rang two days later. It was Tom Friel.

"Everything all right?" I asked anxiously.

"Sure, everything's fine, except these damned clothes," Tom said. "I'm calling you from a public booth because we don't want to take any chances. But here's the story, Eliot. I think we've got just about all we need to know."

Swiftly his voice rolled on.

"We've seen Ralph Capone in the Montmartre, and he seems to do most of his phoning from a telephone in an alcove just behind the bar. The joint is run by a guy named Percy Haller—and don't let that first name fool you. He's a rough gent. The terminal box is on a pole in the alley but there are always some plug-uglies on guard, front and back, day and night."

"Anything else?" I said.

"Not much, except that Marty has struck up an acquaintance with a hood named Tony Marino, who isn't exactly my idea of the All-American boy. But nobody seems to give us any extra attention."

"Okay," I told him. "You and Marty will have to keep on with the masquerade while I try to figure out what to do."

Tom's sigh was audible over the wire.

"All right, Eliot, but I sure hope it doesn't take long. Y'know what? This babe I'm with keeps talking about getting married."

The smile this produced didn't last long as I tried to decide how to make the wire tap possible. Rain beating against the windows matched the drumming of my fingers on the desk. First, we had to get a room in the neighborhood from which to run our listening post. Then we had to lure those guards out of the alley while we racked the board on the terminal box pole and bridged the two terminals.

I phoned my friend Harrison at the telephone company and asked him to lend me a pair of lineman's spikes. I also asked him to check the records of the area in which the Montmartre was located and advise me of the boundaries of the master terminal.

Robsky was in my office when Harrison called back.

"I figured you were making a wire tap," Harrison said. "Well, this will be a tough one because on that type of terminal box you'll have to have someone talking whose voice you recognize so that you can join the exact two terminals. There must be a hundred and fifty terminals on that one—and it's quite a trick."

I thanked him and told Robsky what he had said. Paul confirmed it.

"He's right, Eliot. I'd have to rack the whole board until I caught a familiar voice. Then it would be only a matter of a minute or so to join them."

Asking Robsky to pick up the lineman spikes, I called Chapman and filled him in on our current project. Then I gave him the boundaries of the area in which we needed a room.

"I'll get us a good spot," Lyle assured me.

The next day, Friel called in again from a public booth.

"Tell Lahart to ask to use that private telephone in the Montmartre occasionally," I advised Tom. "I want him to use it enough so that one of these fine days, when I have to hear his voice on it at a certain time, nobody will be suspicious when he asks to use it for a few minutes."

The plan was taking shape in my mind now.

If Lahart were able to use the Montmartre telephone, and if we could lure the guards away from the alley, then we'd be able to do it. But it all had to go off like clockwork, and I had to give Lahart time to make his use of that private telephone an ordinary occurrence.

During the next few days we followed up a lead which Seager and Leeson had discovered, and raided another big brewery that yielded two more five-ton trucks and equipment valued at more than one hundred thousand dollars. We used our established pattern, trapping six men inside by blocking every exit and then crashing through the front doors with our steel-bumpered truck.

The reports of our raid had hardly been filed when Lahart called in from a Cicero drug store to tell me that he was now accepted at the Montmartre as a regular customer with the privilege of using the private phone.

"Nobody says a word when I give 'em the word that I'd like to call a babe from the Capone alcove," he said. "Now, what's up?"

"We're going to try to run the tap tomorrow," I told him. "Robsky has got to get up that pole behind the Montmartre, and when he racks the board he's going to have to hear your voice to know that he has the right plug."

"My part is easy," Marty replied. "Just let me know what time you want my dulcet tones on the air."

I had been toying with a plan to lure the guards away from the alley behind the Montmartre: it depended on our men being seen. I set the time for four o'clock the following afternoon.

"Here's the number of the telephone at the room we have rented," I told Lahart. "Call that number at four o'clock tomorrow and just keep saying sweet nothings so that Robsky can recognize your voice and pick out the proper terminals."

"I'll be on the line," Marty promised. "But tell Chapman not to take me serious when I start making love to him over the wire. Tell him, too, he's the ugliest 'babe' I ever talked to on or off the telephone."

The wheels started to grind quickly. Gathering Chapman and Robsky in my office, together with Seager, Gardner, Cloonan and Leeson, we went over our plans in detail.

"We have to draw those guards away from the alley where the terminal box is located," I told them.

One of the cars we often used on our raids was a Cadillac touring car.

"Jim," I said to Leeson, "I want you to put the top down so that you'll be recognized easily. Then at about three-forty-five tomorrow afternoon, you, Sam, Bill and Barney drive slowly past the Montmartre a couple of times and then start circling around the Western Hotel. You should pick up quite a convoy in no time at all, and when you do, just keep them busy a couple of blocks away from the Montmartre as long as you can."

They nodded and I turned to Robsky.

"Paul, you and I will be down that alley a ways at three-fifty-five. We should be able to watch the guards without being spotted ourselves, and if Leeson and the others manage to draw them off, we'll get to the pole and you'll go up and try to join those terminals. I'll stand watch for you at the bottom, because if they come back too soon you'd be in big trouble."

"Comforting to have you aboard," Robsky put in.

Looking at Chapman, I said:

"Lyle, you've got the toughest job of all—and all my sympathy. "You'll have to sit there in our new wire tap room and listen to Lahart make a pitch at you as if you were a woman."

Chapman laughed.

"It should be kind of funny. I'm anxious to hear what kind of a line Marty hands out."

Fortunately, the next afternoon was crisp and clear. Otherwise, Leeson and his detail might have looked a bit foolish riding around in a touring car with the top down.

At three-fifty Robsky and I parked our car a block from the alley behind the Montmartre. His spikes wrapped in a piece of brown paper, Paul and I ducked into the dark, trash-littered alleyway between a delicatessen and a tailor shop which bisected the alley behind the Montmartre. We both wore rubber-soled shoes and despite the debris cluttering the narrow alleyway we made our way quietly to the intersection.

My watch showed it to be four minutes to four when I peered around the corner and looked toward the rear of the Montmartre, just half a block away.

Only one man was there, but I knew by the pearl gray hat that he was one of Ralph Capone's guards. His back was to me and he stood beside a new Ford coupé facing in our direction.

Even as I watched, the back door of the Montmartre ripped open and a second man ran out and spoke with great agitation and much arm-waving to the man who had been standing outside. Quickly they jumped into the car and roared down the alley toward us.

Jerking back, I motioned to Robsky and we both flattened against the wall. I was glad that this alleyway, because of the high buildings on each side and its bare three-foot width, was so dark, for they didn't even catch a glimpse of us as they sped by.

The bait was working. Leeson and his squad in the touring car were attracting all the attention I had hoped they would.

While I had been scouting the alley, Robsky had strapped on the needle-pointed climbing spikes and belted on the waist strap which would leave his hands free when he was on the pole.

"Let's go," I said, and we sprinted down the alley to the pole behind the Montmartre.

The spikes rasped into the wood as Paul swarmed up the

pole. I watched as he opened the door of the square black terminal box and began to rack the board. A quick look at my watch showed that it was just four o'clock.

Looking up again, I saw Robsky working furiously on the board, his fingers flying over the terminals. Then he leaned sideways against the broad leather belt which was looped around the pole and shook his head negatively.

"Run over it again," I called urgently through my cupped hands.

There was no telling how long our luck might hold out. At any moment those hoods might drive back into the alley or someone might come out the back door of the Montmartre.

Every passing second seemed like an hour, with Paul outlined against the sky at the top of the pole. I slipped my revolver out from its shoulder holster and checked it, drawing some comfort from its solid, familiar feel. Again I checked my watch. Three minutes past four.

Again I looked upward, after checking both ends of the alley for the thousandth time, and saw Paul's fingers freeze in one spot. Then he leaned over, grinning, and gave me the okay sign with circled thumb and forefinger.

It was only a matter of seconds for him to make the bridge. There was a sharp click as he closed the door of the terminal box and then the rasping sounds of descending spikes, welcome music to my ears.

"Okay, it's all finished," he said as he hit the ground. I pushed him ahead of me toward the little alleyway from which we had come.

"Let's get out of here," I said. "We've pressed our luck too much already."

"That's the truth," Paul agreed as we paused briefly while he stripped off the leg spikes. "I felt like first prize at a turkey shoot while I was up there."

Driving back to my office, I was elated over our success. When Leeson and his "bait detail" reported in, I was almost triumphant.

"Eliot, we had such a convoy it looked like a parade," he chuckled. "They couldn't figure out what we were up to and they must have had every hood in town on our tail."

"They certainly put the two most important ones on you, as far as Robsky and I were concerned," I told them. "And thanks for keeping them out of our hair. Maybe now we'll be able to give them something else to think about."

With this new wire tap, I felt confident that we were in a stronger position than ever. But goose pimples skated up and down my spine when I considered what might have happened if Robsky and I had been trapped in the alley behind the Montmartre.

CHAPTER 11

Our wire tap on the Montmartre Café proved vastly informative and highly interesting at times.

Ralph Capone, we learned, usually went there in the late afternoon or evening. Since there would now be a brief lull in our raiding activities as various teams tracked down new leads, I decided to help man the listening post in Cicero.

Chapman was there to greet us with a flourish when Basile and I arrived next afternoon.

"Welcome to the Montmartre subdivision," he said, arms open wide. "There's no beer in the icebox, but I have an instrument here with which we can order some."

He pointed to the telephone headset perched on a small table with a large yellow pad and several sharpened pencils beside it. I took in the rest of the room with a glance.

"Not gaudy but neat enough," I complimented Lyle and then, nodding toward the headset asked, "Has there been any action on the Alexander Graham Bell?"

"Nothing important," he answered. "But there sure was

a heap of conversation last night about why Leeson and the boys were rolling around the Western Hotel. That's about all, though. Just speculation on what we were up to."

I told Chapman that I would take over now and that I had arranged for Mike King to relieve me later.

"Speaking of King," Chapman said, leafing through the pile of newspapers scattered on the bed, "there's a picture of 'Legs' Diamond here in the papers and I'll be damned if he doesn't look just like Mike."

Lyle handed the picture to me. It looked exactly like the wiry little man who was proving a genius at tailing suspects.

"We'll have to call him 'Legs,' " I told Chapman, and the nickname stuck to Mike thereafter.

Lyle was still chuckling as he left. Basile soon was sending deep snores echoing through the room as he slept peacefully in one of the overstuffed chairs.

I paced back and forth, too restless to read, while Basile's deep snores echoed through the room. Constantly my eyes swept to the telephone. It was a peculiar feeling, waiting for the buzz that would indicate a phone call at the Montmartre. I watched it like a man waiting for a time bomb to explode.

After more than an hour I finally settled down to read the newspapers. No sooner had I relaxed than the sharp buzzing of the phone brought me up out of my chair.

Basile's eyes snapped open as I snatched up the headset and clamped it to my head. A harsh, grating voice pounded against my eardrums.

" 'Ello, who's this?"

A heavy, guarded voice replied:

"Haller. Who you want?"

That would be the manager of the Montmartre, character-ized by Friel as a "rough gent." Then the caller demanded:

"Tony there?"

"Yeah, hold on."

After a short wait, a breezy voice said:

"This is Tony. Who's this?"

That would be Tony Marino, the hood Friel had de-scribed. The ensuing conversation proved that Friel was a good judge of bad character.

"This is Bingo," growled the caller. "That broad sure played us for a sucker last night, y'know it? Wadja hav'ta git so God-damned drunk for?"

Tony cut in heatedly.

"Now wait a second, Bingo. You got pretty loaded, too, y'know. Anyhow, I was sure we could both jump this broad. Damned if I know how she got away from us."

"She give us the runaround and I don't take that from no dame," Bingo interjected. "You line her up for us tonight again, y'hear. We'll take her out and she'll lay both of us or I'll knock her God-damned teeth out."

Tony's voice was placating when he answered. This Bingo must be a tough character, I thought. For Tony said:

"Sure, Bingo. Sure. I'll have her meet us here at eight o'clock. This time we'll score for sure. Both of us."

Bingo sounded satisfied now.

"Okay. We'll take her up to my room and take turns. See ya."

The phone clicked and I shook my head. Some woman was in for a rough night of it, but I figured she had to expect it when she played in a league like that one.

Basile had gone back to sleep meanwhile, and when Marty

Lahart dropped in a few minutes later, I filled him in on the conversation I had overheard between his "pal" Marino and the fellow named "Bingo."

"I don't know this Bingo character," Marty said. "But Marino thinks he's a wheel with the ladies. Maybe he is, if he has some plug-ugly to hold them for him."

It was getting dark now, and as I switched on the lights the buzzer signaled another call at the Montmartre. This time it was a woman's voice, far off and syrupy.

"New Orleans calling for Mr. Ralph Capone."

"Just a minute," said the heavy voice I recognized as Haller's.

Then a firm, businesslike voice was in my ear.

"This is Ralph Capone."

"Just a moment please, Mr. Capone. New Orleans calling."

"Hello, Ralph?" said a scratchy voice in the distance. "This is Patsy."

"Yes, Patsy. What's on your mind?"

The distant voice flowed on fawningly.

"Ralph, I just wanted to let you know that it's all fixed in the third race down here tomorrow. It'll be Horse Fly at twenty to one. Can you hear me?"

"Are you sure it's all set?" asked Capone.

"Absolutely, Ralph. I'm betting five gees myself. I'm absolutely positive."

"Well, you better be," Capone said flatly. "I'll put fifteen gees on it. Horse Fly in the third. Right?"

"Right," said the faraway voice.

"Okay, thanks for calling."

A sharp click broke the connection even before "Patsy" could reply.

Hanging up the headset, I turned to Lahart and Basile with a grin:

"I can give you gentlemen a solid gold, bona fide, guaranteed, sure-fire, positive tip on a horse that can't lose tomorrow in the third race at New Orleans."

"You're kidding," Marty answered.

"Not a bit," I replied. "Some gent named Patsy just called Ralph Capone all the way from New Orleans to tip him that it's a sure 'fix.' So sure that this Patsy is betting five thousand on it and Capone is wagering a little matter of fifteen thousand dollars. And when Capone puts that much folding money on it, that horse better win or I'll make a little wager that somebody is in dire trouble."

Marty looked thoughtful. Then his face brightened.

"Say, Eliot, what do you say if we just put a little bet on it, too. I'm not in the habit of getting tips that are this good."

"Why not?" I agreed. "Do you know where we can get a bet down."

"Son," Marty chuckled, "you forget that I have just come from a brief but very intimate sojourn in the underworld. At the moment I can get you just about anything but a brewery."

This was only Thursday, unfortunately. We didn't get paid until late Friday afternoon. Among the three of us—leaving us without lunch money for the next day—we were able to raise the magnificent total of ten dollars.

"So we'll eat big tomorrow night," I quipped. "This horse is a twenty-to-one shot, which means we'll win two hundred dollars."

Marty took the money and left, whistling. A short time later, King came in to relieve me and Basile drove me home.

Friday always entailed a tremendous amount of paper work and I forgot all about our bet on Horse Fly in the third at New Orleans. But Marty hadn't.

It was late in the day when I picked up my telephone to hear him grumbling on the other end.

"What do you know, Eliot. I just called up one of my newspaper friends in the sports department of the *Tribune* and guess what happened. Horse Fly ran absolutely dead last!"

"You're kidding," I told him.

His voice was morbidly emphatic.

"No, sir. That's the straight dope."

"Well, son," I told him. "Let that be a lesson to you not to bet on the horses. And, while you're at it, you might say a brief prayer for Patsy in New Orleans."

I can't say whether there was any connection. But I wasn't surprised to see a small two-paragraph item two days later on one of the inside pages of the *Tribune*. Chicago had seen so much of this kind of thing that it couldn't get overly excited when it happened so far away.

The story simply said that the bodies of two small-time gangsters, riddled with bullets, had been found in a ditch on the outskirts of New Orleans.

I couldn't help wondering whether one of them was "Patsy." Or whether they were the ones who failed to deliver the "fix" that had cost Ralph Capone fifteen thousand dollars—and us the huge sum of ten dollars.

In the room the next day, I found several dividends on

hand. Robsky, who was manning the post, handed me two sheets of recorded conversation written in his bold, firm hand. One sheet read:

"Hello. Let me talk to Ralph."

"Ralph speaking."

"This is McCoy."

"Yes, Mac."

"I've got two real big orders I want to place."

"You know I don't take orders here. Call Guzik at the Wabash Hotel."

"Okay, thanks."

This meant that Jake "Greasy Thumb" Guzik, treasurer of the Capone syndicate, was the boss order taker.

The other sheet Robsky handed me was considerably more exciting. The handwriting leaped out at me.

"Hello, Ralph?"

"Just a minute."

"This is Ralph."

"This is Fusco."

"Yes, Joe."

"I think it's safe now to reopen that spot on South Wabash Avenue."

"Well, I don't know how safe it is, but if you think so, go ahead."

"Okay. What do you hear from Snorky?"

"Not much new. He'll be back soon."

"Okay, I'll go ahead with the South Wabash Avenue deal."

"All right. Keep in touch."

I read it over several times. "Snorky," I knew, was the nickname close associates used for Al Capone. The reference to him meant that he would soon be in town.

The "South Wabash Avenue deal" referred to one of their finest breweries, one we had closed. Apparently, they were going to try to reopen it.

Phoning Chapman immediately, I told him to put a round-the-clock watch on that site for a few days.

Three days later, Mike King called me from a rooming house in that neighborhood.

"You had the right dope, Eliot," he said. "They spent all night moving equipment into that warehouse. It ought to be in operation in two or three days."

"That's fine," I told him. "You can drop off there now that we know it's going to be running."

Late Friday night I gathered my crew together, and we raided the plant on South Wabash Avenue. We did it just as we had the first time, covering all exits so that no one escaped, and crashing through the front doors in our truck. This time we arrested six men, took two trucks and destroyed beer and equipment valued at one hundred thousand dollars.

Thus, four nights after the Capone syndicate had tried to reopen one of the first breweries we closed down, we had put it out of business again and cost them a huge amount of money in the bargain.

All the difficulty in establishing the wire tap on the Montmartre had already paid much greater dividends than I had dared to expect.

The next evening, however, somebody tried to pay me off in bullets.

I had accepted an invitation to have dinner with Betty and her parents, and after dinner she suggested that we take a ride.

It was a cloudy night, but we were enjoying a slow drive

through the countryside until I noticed a pair of headlights fixed steadily in my rear-view mirror.

Aimlessly, so as not to alarm Betty, I made several turns. The lights were still there!

"Let's stop somewhere and chat a little while," Betty suggested.

I tried to control my agitation, fighting back the vision of our car being riddled by machine gun fire. With great effort, I kept my voice level and inserted a note of regret.

"I'm terribly sorry, honey, but I do have to get back to the office in very short order. I was just about to tell you that I'll have to be heading back right now."

She gave me a long, searching look and smiled her understanding. Careful not to show my anxiety, I drove swiftly back to her house, keeping a wary eye on the rear-view mirror all the way. Just before we arrived, those headlights disappeared from view.

I wondered, as I walked her to the door and quickly kissed her good night, whether I had been imagining things. The neighborhood was deserted; there wasn't a car in sight. Nerves, I told myself.

Relaxing, I hardly noticed the parked car facing in the opposite direction. But as I approached to within a few yards of it, there was a bright flash from the front window, and I ducked instinctively as my windshield splintered in tune with the bark of a revolver. Without thinking, I jammed the accelerator to the floor. As my car leaped ahead, there was another flash, and the window of my left rear door was smashed by another slug.

The tires squealed as I hurtled around the next corner. Thank God Betty wasn't with me. But the realization that she might have been sitting just where the first bullet pierced the windshield sent a cold rage surging through me. Driving madly, I circled the block, taking my gun from the shoulder holster and holding it in my left hand as I doubled back to get behind the car which had ambushed me. Now I wanted my turn, but the would-be assassin had faded into the night.

Only the uncertain lighting and my sudden acceleration had saved me. I wondered, as I drove back into the city with my gun on my lap, whether this attempt to kill me had been ordered or whether it had been planned as a "welcome home" present for "Scarface Al." Perhaps it was a personal bit of enterprise by someone like the sneering pearl gray hat of the elevator.

One thing was certain: someone had declared open season on Eliot Ness, and it was a damned uncomfortable feeling.

Chapter 12

We had been in the brewery-busting business almost six months when the prison gates swung open at Holmesburg, Pennsylvania, and Al Capone walked out a free man on the morning of March 17, 1930.

There was wild excitement in Chicago as the public and the underworld awaited the homecoming of the scarfaced chieftain who ruled the city with an iron fist in a glove of steel.

Speculation was rife as to what he was going to do, how the gangs of Chicago would react to his return and what sort of reception was being planned by the city and federal governments. The newspapers devoted lurid black headlines to the story.

Chicago officials had been making eye-catching statements as the time drew near for Capone's release. The law promised he would be given a hot reception.

"We'll clap him in jail as soon as he sets foot in the city," boasted one high police figure.

Captain John Stege, head of the Chicago detective bureau, posted twenty-five men in the vicinity of Capone's home on Prairie Avenue. Their instructions were to take the chubby-faced gang overlord into custody as soon as he arrived, but they waited four days and nights without avail.

"Scarface Al" had apparently disappeared into thin air after being met at the prison by a "royal" entourage that whisked him out of sight. Since there was no indictment against him, however, the police obviously weren't too anxious to locate him.

But we knew immediately where he was, thanks to the wire tap on the Montmartre.

When word came that Capone had disappeared, I laid siege to the headset in our rented basement apartment.

One of the first orders of business among the mob when he returned, I knew, would be the extermination of the Eliot Ness squad which had become a thorn in Al's pasty white side. The orders, I was fairly certain, would filter through brother Ralph's telephone.

On March 18, the day after Capone's release, I was at the headset when the buzzer sounded and an urgent voice demanded:

"Is Ralph there?"

"On the phone," was the reply.

"Listen, Ralph," the voice pleaded frantically. "We're up in Room 718 in the Western and Al is really getting out of hand. He's in terrible shape. Will you come up, please? You're the only one who can handle him when he gets like this. We've sent for a lot of towels."

"Okay," Ralph replied. "I'll be up a little later. Just take care of things the best you can right now."

Without question, Al Capone, celebrating his release from prison not wisely but much too well, was drunk and almost out of control up in Room 718 at the Western Hotel. I didn't know what the towels were for, whether to wet him down or clean him up, but it was obvious that Ralph wasn't worried.

About fifteen minutes after that call, the buzzer sounded again.

"Ralph," said the caller, "this is Jake Lingle. Where's Al? I've been looking all over for him and nobody seems to know where he is."

Ralph pretended ignorance.

"I don't know where he is, either, Jake," he hedged. "I haven't heard a word from him since he got out."

Lingle, a Chicago *Tribune* police reporter, sounded agitated and I marveled at his effrontery.

"Jesus, Ralph, this makes it very bad for me. I'm supposed to have my finger on these things, y'know. It makes it very embarrassing with my paper. Now get this, I want you to call me the minute you hear from him. Tell him I want to see him right away."

"All right," Ralph replied. "I will."

Within an hour, Lingle called Ralph again.

"Ralph?"

"Yes."

"This is Jake again. Have you heard from Al yet?"

"No. Not yet."

Lingle's voice became aggressively indignant.

"Listen, you guys ain't giving me the runaround, are you? Just remember, I wouldn't do that if I was you."

Ralph's voice became a bit warmer and friendlier.

"Now, Jake, you know I wouldn't do that. It's just that I haven't heard from Al. What else can I tell you?"

"Okay, okay," Lingle growled. "Just remember to tell him that I want to talk to him right away."

The phone banged down and I wondered what reason Lingle had to play it so high and mighty with the Capones.

Four days after his return from prison, Capone finished up his celebration. Defying the law to pin anything on him, he walked blithely into police headquarters accompanied by his lawyer.

"I hear you want me," Capone challenged.

No one did, as it developed, and "Scarface Al" returned in triumph to his headquarters at the Lexington Hotel, where he occupied the three top floors.

It was an ironic demonstration of the power of this man who had started out as a hardfisted roughneck addicted to red neckties, gaudy shirts and flashy jewelry.

His fortune was estimated at $50,000,000. He rode around in a $30,000 automobile which, with its body armor of steel plate and bulletproof windows, weighed seven tons. He owned an estate in Florida worth $500,000, and on one meaty finger he wore an eleven-carat diamond which had cost $50,000. Capone never carried less than $50,000 in cash, scattering $25 tips to hat check girls and $100 gratuities to waiters. He was known around the gambling spots as "a sucker for the ponies."

But those who took him for a "sucker" elsewhere usually wound up dead. Acquiring the poise which comes with power, Capone had become even more dangerous: together with his ruthlessness, he had the quality of a great business-man. Under that patent leather hair he had sound judgment, diplomatic shrewdness and the diamond-hard nerves of a gambler, all balanced by cold common sense.

He had always been a fighter, this man who scorned the law, but even more deadly was the fact that he held with the Sicilian tradition of secret murder. Catching an enemy off guard was the cornerstone of his strategy. Rarely did hate actuate him; when it did, however, those who had incurred his wrath were marked for death.

We weren't going to be caught off guard if I could help it. To prepare for an emergency, I decided to make a survey of the area around his Lexington headquarters.

Taking Lahart with me, I had Basile drive us around the block several times while we charted the exits, parking areas and alleyways.

As we swung past the main entrance, a hoodlum named Frank Foster, alias Frankie Frost, who acted as a liaison man between Capone and "Bugs" Moran, swaggered out of the lobby. We were almost face to face through the car window for a fleeting second, and from his startled expression I knew that he had recognized me.

Looking back, I saw him stare after us for a moment, then hurry across the street and leap into a parked car facing in the opposite direction.

"Swing it around fast, Frank," I tapped Basile on the shoulder, "and follow the black sedan just pulling out behind the bread truck."

Foster swung left at the first intersection, and we could see him peering back. Then his car shot forward in an effort to lose us.

"Get him, Frank," I urged. "Swing him into the curb."

The chase covered two miles as we raced block after block

through crowded city streets, the speedometer flicking past sixty miles an hour. Careening around corners, weaving between cars, ignoring traffic lights and scattering pedestrians with a blaring horn, we missed disaster several times by a matter of inches.

Basile, hunched over the wheel with cold concentration, finally drew abreast of Foster's sedan. The gangster threw us a wide-eyed stare as we shot ahead of him and then, with a quick wrench of the wheel accompanied by a shrieking of rubber and a squealing of breaks, we slued in front to force the sedan to the curb.

Lahart and I leaped from the car before it had stopped rolling. Sprinting back as Marty raced to the other side of Foster's car, I wrenched open the door. Foster shrank back as I pushed my revolver into his face. Reaching in, I grabbed a handful of coat, dragged him out of the car and slammed him up against the side of the sedan.

"Make one move and you'll wish you hadn't," I said.

But Foster, a swarthy, hard-faced man of about five feet, eight inches, wasn't ready to act as tough as he looked. He was shaking as his hands shot meekly into the air. Jamming my pistol into his midriff, I searched him quickly.

From a hand-tooled shoulder holster under the left armpit of his dapper pin-striped suit, I lifted a snub-nosed .38 Colt revolver exactly like the one I had pointed at his diamond-studded belt buckle.

Strangely enough, I noted as the excitement of the chase ebbed and I looked around to take my bearings, we had brought him to heel right in front of the Transportation Building where our offices were located.

"Now we'll go up to my office and talk awhile," I told

Foster, putting away my gun and pocketing his. "And don't get any funny ideas about making a break for it."

Foster marched docilely between us, but once assured that he wasn't going to receive rough physical treatment, remained firmly silent when we questioned him about Capone and the rackets.

"I don't have to say nothin'," he repeated over and over, so after a fruitless half hour we turned him in on a gun-carrying charge.

There had been frequent gang murders in the few months preceding "Scarface Al's" return. A serious breach was threatening to disrupt the "peace treaty" Capone had negotiated at Atlantic City. Meanwhile, the Secret Six had established the nation's first large-scale crime detection laboratory at Northwestern University.

I had met Major Calvin Goddard, the ballistics expert in charge of the laboratory, and on a hunch I decided to drive out to Evanston and show him the gun I had taken from Foster.

Goddard's big body was hunched over a microscope as I walked into a laboratory crammed with steel files and numerous glass-fronted cases. His dark hair was rumpled and a shoulder holster was pushed around to the center of his back so it wouldn't interfere with his arms as he worked.

The major was never without a gun, even in the privacy of his laboratory on the quiet Northwestern campus. There was a tremendous amount of damning material stored in those bulging files, and so bold were the gangsters who infested Chicago that even this serene spot wasn't completely safe from an invasion aimed at the destruction of evidence.

Peering at me through thick-rimmed glasses, the major

waved his recognition, his deep voice hearty as he said:

"Be with you in a second, Eliot."

He straightened up and shook hands with a hard, firm grip.

"Just ran a test on a bullet fired from a gun we picked up and found out it's the same gun used in a killing on the South Side a couple of months ago," he told me in the manner of a proud parent recounting a child's cute saying.

Reaching into my topcoat pocket, I pulled out the gun I had taken from Foster and handed it to him.

"Major, I'm not quite certain just how this ballistics business works, but I thought maybe you'd like to look at this gun I picked up from a punk named Frank Foster."

Goddard took it, examined it and checked to make certain it was loaded.

"Come here," he directed. "I'll show you exactly how it works."

Moving to a large wastebasket solidly packed with cotton waste, he fired into the wadding. The sound of the shot reverberated through the room like summer thunder. He was digging into the waste for the expended bullet when a uniformed guard poked his head through the doorway and made a quick inspection of the room.

"It's okay, George. Just running a test," Goddard grunted.

The guard flicked his hand in a semisalute and withdrew.

"We take our precautions," the major said, jerking his head toward the door. "Now, look, here's the way this thing works."

He placed the bullet under his microscope and adjusted the lens.

"Take a look through there and you'll see lines along the

side of the bullet which were left by the rifling of the pistol barrel." I peered into the microscope and saw these long scratches. "Every pistol's rifling varies somewhat so that by comparing two bullets you can tell whether or not they were shot from the same weapon," he added.

He then went on to explain how a bullet taken from a body could be compared with a test bullet from a gun taken from a suspect to determine whether the pistol carried by the suspect had fired the killing shot.

When I was ready to leave, Goddard picked up the bullet he had fired from the Foster gun and dropped it into an envelope. His voice sounded eager.

"I'll check this against some of the bullets in our unsolved file. But whether I can match it or not, I'll keep this one on file in case this gun ever pops up again."

I dropped the Foster gun into my topcoat pocket, drove back to my office in the Transportation Building and locked the revolver in one of the drawers of the steel filing cabinets where we kept our own records.

I could see already that the return of Capone was having a marked influence on us. We were so few against so many, and the arrogant theatrics of "Scarface Al's" homecoming boasted to the world that he had lost little, if any, of his murderous power. It made you feel like a sitting duck in a shooting gallery.

Chapter 13

Immediately following the gangster chief's homecoming, I put increased pressure on my men to uncover several more breweries. They didn't need my prodding, but perhaps I was overeager to show Capone that times and types had changed.

With the unbeatable tactics we had now developed into a science, we cost him another two hundred and fifty thousand dollars in beer, equipment and trucks by wiping out two more breweries. We also took five men into custody, which meant that the bail bond fees were mounting into staggering totals, too. But the next two raids uncovered nothing but dry holes, with obvious indications that the breweries had been hastily moved.

"I can't understand it," I told Lahart as we tried to figure out how the mob could have known in advance about our raids.

Pondering the question, I found myself looking intently at

the telephone. Suddenly it occurred to me that if we could tap their phones, wasn't it possible that they could have tapped ours?

Going downstairs to a public booth, I called Harrison at the telephone company and asked him to run a thorough check on my line.

It was exactly as I suspected.

He called back later to say that he had cleared our lines and would run a check each week.

A telephone company investigation showed that several telephone workers had recently left their jobs and "gone over to the syndicate for bigger money," he told me. He had also learned, from a friend of one of those who had left, that the syndicate employed a crew of union electricians to assist their telephone experts.

"But we're on to them now, and we'll make certain that you aren't bothered any more," he promised.

Yet, a few weeks later two more raids proved futile. A check showed that our telephones were clear of taps.

I was puzzling over this newest problem when the "Kid" strutted into my office, and from his manner I knew that he had something out of the ordinary on his mind. As he settled into a chair and went through the usual routine of adjusting his sharply creased trousers, the telephone rang.

"Boss," Basile informed me from the outer office, "I just thought you'd like to know the Kid's got another new car. It's a big splashy job that must of set him back a chunk."

"Fine," I replied. "Thanks."

Turning to the "Kid" I said: "Let's see how much money you have in that getaway fund."

He protested momentarily and then, realizing that I was

adamant, pulled out the Postal Savings deposit book. It showed a five-hundred-dollar balance and no recent withdrawals of any large amount.

"They're treating you fairly well, huh?" I asked him.

"Can't kick," he answered expansively.

The young man's blitheness never failed to stagger me. He was sitting astride a power keg, playing both ends against the middle and yet he seemed not to be aware that he lived in a dream world which might turn suddenly into a nightmare. My voice was gruff as I held his eyes with mine.

"Today I want some information. And I want straight answers."

He recognized the uncompromising tone and shifted uncomfortably in his chair.

"We've made a couple of raids lately," I snapped. "When we got there the places had been cleaned out, lock, stock and barrel. What I want to know is, how come? Where are they getting their information?"

An injured look came into his eyes; he shook his head vigorously from side to side.

"Search me. Honest to God, Mr. Ness, I don't know where they got the information. But I can tell you one thing."

"What's that?"

"Well, since the boss man got back, the word has gone out that anybody who finds out that you are watching a certain brewery and tips off the mob gets a fast five-hundred-dollar reward," he said. "That means a lot of people must be looking at you whenever your guys leave this office."

It made sense. In the two most recent instances someone had probably recognized one of our men and relayed the information to the mob.

Fidgeting in his chair, the "Kid" coughed nervously. I knew that something important was on his mind.

"Okay, what is it?" I demanded.

He reached into his inside coat pocket and pulled out a plain envelope.

"Mr. Ness," he began uneasily, "I don't want you to get mad at me. I told them it wouldn't do any good but they told me to try it anyhow. So I gotta try."

Jerking upright, he slid the envelope onto the desk in front of me and then retreated hastily into his chair. I folded back the unsealed flap and came out with two crackling, brand new notes.

Each one was a thousand-dollar bill.

Momentarily hypnotized, I sat there staring down at the first thousand-dollar bills I had ever seen. From a distance I heard the "Kid" saying:

"They said that if you'll take it easy, you'll get the same amount—two thousand dollars—each and every week."

I could feel the anger rising in my chest and reached out to take a viselike grip on my throat. My jaws locked so tightly that my teeth ached; the fingers holding the bills started to shake and I knew, as I jammed the bills back into the envelope and looked up at the "Kid," that my face was a distorted mask. He pushed back in his chair as I rose from my chair and held his arms out in front of him like a man warding off a blow.

"Don't hit me, Mr. Ness," he choked. "I didn't mean to do this but they made me. Honest they did. I told them it wasn't any use trying."

Fighting to get hold of myself, I walked around the desk and stood in front of him. Slowly I reached down, pulled him up out of the chair and, opening his jacket, stuffed the envelope back into his inner pocket. My voice sounded strange.

"Listen—and listen carefully," I told him. "I want you to take this envelope back to them and tell them that Eliot Ness can't be bought—not for two thousand a week, ten thousand or a hundred thousand. Not for all the money they'll ever lay their scummy hands on."

The "Kid" started backing toward the door.

"Tell them they'll never understand it," I growled, almost to myself.

White faced, the "Kid" had the door half open when I stopped him. He flinched as I walked toward him.

"Get this straight," I glared. "Make damned sure that that money gets back to the person who gave it to you. I mean *all* of it. Because if I ever find out that you kept it, so help me God I'll break you into tiny pieces with my bare hands."

Gulping audibly, the "Kid" held up his right hand like a man taking an oath.

"I swear it, Mr. Ness. I swear it."

With that, the door banged behind him. The flood of anger was receding now, and I turned back to my desk.

With the "boss man" back, the first step was bribery. What next?

That night my car was stolen again. I wondered, as I called Betty and broke another date and took a taxi home, whether it would be found this time or whether it would disappear as completely as Marty's had.

Next morning the indignant Basile popped in to tell me that it had been found abandoned on the South Side.

"Only one thing, boss," he fumed. "The bastards who took

it also took the front wheels off of it. I had to get it towed into the garage."

Nuisance retaliation! They still hadn't given up their hopes of diminishing the efficiency of my outfit through bribery. This was clear later that morning when Lahart and Seager burst into my office. Marty was volubly incredulous.

"Chief," he gasped, "those monkeys tried to buy us off."

I listened with interest as he told me how he and Seager had been tracking a load of barrels from the cleaning plant at 38th and Shields.

"Sam's driving down the street about two blocks behind the load, and as far as we can tell there isn't a convoy with the barrel truck this time," Marty was saying. "All of a sudden—zoom, there's the Ford coupé right beside us and one of the pearl gray hats flips something into our car. It sails right past Sam's nose and lands right in my lap."

Sam bit the end off a cigar and his head disappeared behind a bluish cloud of smoke as he lit up while Marty continued breathlessly.

"Well, I thought for a second maybe we were on the receiving end of a pineapple. But what am I holding but a roll of bills big enough to choke a horse!"

Marty chuckled.

"Sam takes one look, sees what it is and says: 'Watch me catch 'em. Then you can give them a lateral pass.' So off we go, and while he's running down that souped-up Ford I make a quick count and as near as I can estimate—because of the way we're bouncing along—there has to be two thousand bucks in that roll."

Nodding, I asked Marty: "Did you catch them?"

"I'll say," he laughed. "Sam came up so close beside them

we'll both need a new paint job. Then I pitched a pass that would have made Frank Carideo of Notre Dame look like a substitute. It hit the monkey who was driving right in the eye—and he almost wrecked both of us."

A new surge of confidence swept through me as I heard Marty's story. These two men earned the sum total of twenty-eight hundred dollars a year. They had been tempted with the better part of a year's salary, yet had scorned a bribe which probably would have been impossible to trace. My voice was gruff.

"At the risk of being awfully corny, I want you guys to know that I'm pretty damned proud of you."

"What the hell, Eliot," Sam said. "We want to beat 'em, not join 'em."

"I've got to admit one thing," Marty interrupted kiddingly. "I had to make three or four swings before I got off that pass. Those bills just didn't seem to want to leave Pappa's hand."

"Bunk," Sam grunted. "You hit that guy on the first peg, and you were so mad I thought you were going right through the window after him."

I told them of the offer which had been made to me through the "Kid," the anger rising in me again as I related the details. Marty let loose a reflective whistle.

"Boy, what they tossed us was just carfare, huh?"

"No," I replied. "They know that's big money to people like us. They just can't understand that some people won't be bought. But sooner or later the idea will simmer through their thick skulls and then, in all probability, they'll try some rough stuff. But it sure is nice to know that my guys can't be bought."

"You can tell the world!" Marty cracked.

143

His words rang in my ears insistently.

Why not? I thought. Why not do just that?—and "tell the world"—and "Scarface Al" Capone—that Eliot Ness and his men couldn't be bought. The idea kept bouncing around inside my head as Marty and Sam filled me in on their progress in trying to locate another brewery.

"That's exactly what we're going to do," I declared.

"What's that?" Sam asked.

"Tell the world, just as Marty suggested. I'm going to make a few calls and then I'm going to take you two to lunch—on the government—to make up in a very minor way for that two thousand dollars you tossed away this morning. Then we're coming back here and 'tell the world.' "

They both looked puzzled. But they got the drift as I leafed through the telephone book and began to call the newspapers and newsreel outfits.

"This is going to ruin my social life in places like the Montmartre," Marty chuckled as I called the *Tribune* and, having attained some notoriety as a "gangbuster," was swiftly put through to the city desk.

"But you'll be a big hero," I joked.

Completing my calls, in which I informed each newspaper and motion-picture company that I was having a "sensational" press conference at two o'clock that afternoon, I took my two men to lunch.

"And," I told them in the elevator, "you can have all you can eat—as long as you take the thirty-five-cent blue-plate special."

There was little conversation as we ate, each busy with his own thoughts. I began to study these two vastly different men —the gusty, irrepressible Lahart and the stolid, unemotional

144

Seager. Why, I wondered, were they in this? In my case, it was a heterogeneous mixture, a passion for police work, a dislike of seeing people abused and, basically, the thrill of action.

"Sam," I finally asked Seager as he waded through a chunk of apple pie, "what made you come into this thing?"

He chewed reflectively for several seconds, his square jaw working steadily, and then laid aside his fork.

"Police work is about all I've ever known, Eliot. I couldn't take that tour of duty in the death house any more. I had to get outside where I could move around and see people who still had some sort of hope. Then this came along and, well, it's quite an experience."

He prodded a piece of crust with his fork and then looked me right in the eye.

"Maybe it'll surprise you, Eliot, but I've always wanted a chicken farm. Now I've seen just about all the trouble I want. If I get through this one—or I guess I should say 'when'—I think I'll settle for that farm."

I was surprised, because I had never pictured Sam as the country type. Yet I was even more astonished when Lahart chimed in solemnly:

"Damned if I know what my reasons were, except that the job in the post office was driving me crazy and I wanted some kicks. But let me tell you, Sam, that farm idea sounds pretty good. Imagine, nothing to worry about but whether the hens are layin'."

It's getting to all of us, I thought as we left the restaurant. It isn't facing danger that cuts you up inside. It's the waiting and the not knowing what's coming.

When we returned to the office, Basile was shrugging off

the questions of more than a dozen reporters and cameramen. Flashbulbs began to pop as we walked in and, raising my hands to quiet them, I told them there would be plenty of time for everything.

"First, let's go into my office and I'll give you the story. Then you can take all the pictures you want."

When they were settled, and while the newsreels were setting up their cameras, I told them of the attempted briberies. I related in detail how an emissary of Capone's had tried to buy me off for two thousand dollars a week and how Marty and Sam had thrown back their flying bribe.

Pencils scribbled rapidly, and there was a rush for telephones. Flashlight bulbs popped incessantly and the story had to be repeated for the motion-picture cameras.

It was a long, wearisome process but well worth the effort. Possibly it wasn't too important for the world to know that we couldn't be bought, but I did want Al Capone and every gangster in the city to realize that there were still a few law enforcement agents who couldn't be swerved from their duty.

As the last group was leaving, I heard one of the men say: "Those guys are dead pigeons."

Pigeons, I thought grimly, who will take a lot of killing. At the very outset I had chosen my men with an eye toward their ability to take care of themselves under almost any conditions. These men were not hoodlums who had all their courage in their trigger finger. They were alert, fearless and extremely fit and capable. They trusted nobody except themselves, and we had long since devised a system of working in pairs. They would be hard to cut down, I knew.

Meanwhile, defiance of the type we had exhibited was unheard of in a racket-infested city where opposition was so consistently bought off or killed off. Our revelation of the bribes was a sensation. The story was splashed across front pages from coast to coast.

One story opened:

Eliot Ness and his young agents have proved to Al Capone that they are untouchable.

A caption writer adopted it for another paper and over our pictures rode the bold, black words:

"THE UNTOUCHABLES"

The wire service picked up the phrase and the words swept across the nation.

So were born "The Untouchables."

Chapter 14

Our public defiance of the Capone mob brought a horde of congratulatory letters from all parts of the nation.

Strangely enough, not all of them were from prohibitionists. One was from Halbert Louis Hoard, editor of the Jefferson County *Union* in Fort Atkinson, Wisconsin.

I had a rare laugh in this period of watchful waiting when I read his words:

Dear Mr. Ness:

I am a one hundred per cent wet, but I honor you for your bravery. The sooner you put those bootlegger drys where they can't vote for prohibition, the quicker we can get a repeal of the Eighteenth Amendment. I'm for you.

Sincerely,
H. L. HOARD

Capone, I knew, could not afford to pass up our challenge. He had to crush us to survive. If he failed, he was doomed.

Again and again I impressed on my men the necessity of traveling in pairs and being ever on the alert. When we went into a restaurant, we always took a corner table so that we could watch the entire room. Every day we ate in a different place to avoid falling into a pattern. Nor did we ever use the same route twice in succession, because habit could make it that much easier for them to plan a fatal ambush.

And I was expecting a killing.

When it came, I was surprised at the victim. For when the guns finally did bark, they cut down Jake Lingle, the police reporter for the Chicago *Tribune,* the same man I had heard on the Montmartre wire tap trying to reach Al Capone through his brother Ralph on the day "Scarface Al" came home from prison.

It was on June 9, 1930, that Lingle had been shot to death shortly after noon in the pedestrian tunnel under Michigan Boulevard while on his way to the Illinois Central railroad station.

The story created as much of a stir as if Capone's gunmen had wiped out the entire band of Untouchables with one murderous fusillade. The Chicago *Tribune* offered a reward of twenty-five thousand dollars, which was matched by the Chicago *Herald-Examiner,* for the capture and conviction of the murderer.

It was supposed, of course, that Lingle had been murdered because of a crusading investigation into the rackets.

Only later was it revealed that he had actually been a liaison man between the racketeers and the world of police and politicians, a go-between who eventually became too arrogant and too greedy. Lingle, drawing down sixty-five dollars a week as a police reporter had a twenty-five thousand dollar summer home at Long Beach, a luxurious West Side apartment, a suite at the Stevens Hotel and a chauffeur-driven limousine.

From various police sources, the information came to me, piece by piece, that Lingle had double-crossed the Moran gang when it paid him fifty thousand dollars to obtain for it the privilege of operating a dog track on the West Side.

At the same time, Lingle had been working hand in glove with the Capone gang. Capone's interests were protected but the price was high; in fact, Lingle didn't turn a hair when he lost seventy-five thousand dollars in the stock market crash. There was always more to be had for the asking.

As the facts unraveled, I was certain that the "Bugs" Moran mob had confronted Lingle with his "double cross." I was also certain that our influence on the Capone income had something to do with the case. Capone had been paying heavily and reports had it that Lingle's demands were greater than ever.

Capone saw an easy way out and withdrew his protection.

I was satisfied with this theory, particularly after I recalled Lingle's desperate conversation with Ralph Capone less than three months earlier. Again I could hear Lingle's threatening voice as he talked to Ralph Capone who, knowing "Scarface Al" was at that very moment in the Western Hotel, denied knowing his whereabouts. Those words of Lingle's ran through my mind:

"Listen, you guys ain't giving me the runaround, are you? Just remember, I wouldn't do that if I was you."

You didn't threaten the Capones, I thought and then froze as I remembered that this was exactly what we were doing. But Lingle needed their protection and we didn't. We made our own. Yes, I was satisfied that Lingle's greed had paved the way for his execution at the hands of the Moran mob— with the sanction of Al Capone.

A few days later I received a call from Pat Roach, chief investigator for the state attorney's office, that changed my thinking.

"What's cooking, Pat?" I asked him casually, hardly suspecting that he was calling about the Lingle case.

"Well, Eliot," he replied, "the gun found beside Lingle's body was identified by a ballistics man as one of five snub-nosed .38's that Frank Foster bought from Peter von Frantzius, a sporting goods dealer out on Diversey Parkway."

The mention of Foster's name snapped me to minute attention.

"I recall that you confiscated a gun from Foster," he continued, "and I have reason to believe that it is one of those which were bought by Foster in that batch. All I wanted to do was make certain that you had it."

"I've got it," I told him.

"Fine," he approved. "Just hang onto it because we may have to check it out."

After he hung up, I went to the private filing cabinet where I had stored the Foster gun. Pulling open the drawer, I stiffened. It was gone! I searched frantically, inspecting all the other drawers. There was no question about it. The gun was gone, although I had the only keys to this cabinet!

Then something else penetrated my consciousness. Some of the other folders in which I kept private records were not in proper order. Somebody had been rifling my files and had taken the revolver!

Fortunately, no irreplaceable records were kept in these

files and a check revealed that, while the files had been inspected thoroughly, nothing else except the gun had been taken.

The Capone gang—for it could be no other—had started to show its hand. They had entered our offices, probably in the dead of night, and searched for evidence that could be destroyed.

Immediately, I contacted Chapman.

"What's wrong?" he asked anxiously, closing the door behind him.

"Somebody—and you can probably guess who just as well as I can—has been looting our files. The Foster gun is gone and I don't know what else."

Panic clutched at me as I remembered all the evidence Lyle had been collecting. I had left the paper work, aiming at a conspiracy charge against Capone, entirely in his keeping. Since he was a master hand at such things and needed no help from me, I rarely checked over his reports.

"Good grief," I exploded. "Look quick and make sure they haven't taken any of your stuff.

I envisioned the mysterious prowler pocketing those records which proved that Capone was tied in with the purchase of beer trucks, so necessary to the conspiracy case, and other damaging evidence showing that he had been receiving money from the sale of beer.

Lyle relieved my mind on that score.

"They couldn't have taken any of those records," he reported. "I keep them fairly up to date, and as soon as they are in shape, I send them right along to the district attorney's office."

"Thank God for that," I burst out.

Then a frown appeared on Chapman's face and he chewed at his lip.

"Now that you mention it," he said finally, "I have noticed minor items disappearing from time to time in the last few weeks. I just thought that they were being lost in the shuffle somewhere. But it looks fairly clear now that we are having visitors in the night."

There was no question in my mind that something drastic would have to be done. Chapman's conscientious work in forwarding his reports and evidence to the United States District Attorney almost as quickly as they were compiled had saved us this time. But now it would be impossible to leave any of our paper work in the office. There was no way of telling how much secret information the Capone mob already had from our files and how much use it had been to them.

Immediately, I made a decision.

"Lyle," I said, "we are going to have to move all of our records out of here and keep any new evidence in a safer place than this. What I think you'd better do is go down to the First National Bank and hire a safety deposit box section."

He nodded his agreement.

"From now on we'll do all our paper work in the safety deposit department of the bank and keep our evidence in the vault. If they get in there, well, we're pretty close to being out of business."

"We were lucky this time," he affirmed. "I'll get on the bank arrangements right away."

As he left, however, I didn't feel very lucky. I couldn't get the idea out of my head that the gun from my files had killed Lingle, that somehow it had been looted from my files and delivered into the hands of the killer who fired the shot into Lingle's head.

I could see the headlines and stories built around my negligence and the inferences that would be drawn.

I was perspiring heavily by this time, so much so that when the "Kid" came into my office a few minutes later I hardly noticed his dapper new outfit complete with glittering patent leather shoes.

"George, in holding those ears of yours close to the ground have you heard any mention of anybody getting in here at night and rifling my files?" I asked him.

His answer was direct and I thought, watching him closely, an honest one.

"Not a thing, Mr. Ness. Did somebody take something important?"

I didn't want anybody, least of all the Capone mob, to know how important I believed that gun to be, for it might give them some new ideas.

"Oh, nothing really important," I said in an attempt to be casual. "It's just that the whole thing is damned annoying."

Switching the subject quickly, I asked if he had any information for me.

He took an envelope with some writing on it out of his inside coat pocket, the same one, I remembered, from which he had taken that two-thousand-dollar bribe offer, and cleared his throat importantly.

"I've got something here I'll bet you're interested in," he squeaked.

"If it concerns Capone, you bet I'm interested," I told him.

Nodding happily, he read off a telephone number.

"That number operates twenty-four hours a day," he said. "It's to be used only to report on the operations of your outfit. There's always somebody at that number and they pass along the information to the right department within the mob."

Noting the number, I ushered the "Kid" out and called Robsky.

"Get through to George Harrison at the telephone company," I told him, reading off the number the "Kid" had given me. "Have him find out the location of this new number for you on the q.t., check up on the location and run me in a wire tap. If it looks like a tough one to make, call me and we'll work something out."

Robsky assured me he would go to work on it immediately and I went back to my desk to brood some more over the missing gun. I was still holding in my hand the scrap of paper on which I had written down the number I had relayed to Robsky. Idly, my fingers worried it into a ball and I flipped it at the wastepaper basket.

The tiny ball of paper struck the rim of the basket and bounched to the floor. Bending down to pick it up, my head was inches from the wastebasket. As I looked down at the bottom, I recalled the wastebasket packed with wadded cotton out at Northwestern University into which Major Goddard had fired the bullet from the Foster revolver.

That was it!

Goddard, who undoubtedly had the Lingle bullet by now, or a photo of it, could tell me whether the bullet had been fired from the Foster gun which was stolen from my files.

"Let's go," I shouted to Basile.

"Where's the fire?" he asked as we plunged into the corridor and rang for the elevator.

"Inside my head," I snapped. "Take me out to the crime lab at Evanston and don't spare the horses."

Frank didn't. We made it in record time, and I dashed into the building and straight into Goddard's sanctum. As usual, his thick spectacles were pushed up on his forehead and the shoulder holster still sagged between his bowed shoulder blades.

"Major," I blurted, "do you still have my bullet?"

He stared at me a moment. Then his frown of concentration lifted.

"Oh, yes, I remember now, Eliot. You mean the bullet from that Foster gun?"

"That's the one."

"Why certainly, Eliot. Once they get into my collection they don't get out again."

"Well, for God's sake, Major, run a check on it and tell me whether that bullet compares with the one which killed Lingle. You do have the Lingle bullet, don't you?"

He nodded,, then turned to a row of files and began flipping through a series of cards. I watched him for what seemed like hours. Finally he went to a cabinet and took out an envelope with a tag on it.

"Your bullet," he said, waving the envelope.

Turning to another cabinet, he withdrew another envelope. His announcement was cryptic.

"Lingle's."

Taking the two bullets, he placed them side by side under the microscope.

It was actually a short wait, I suppose, before he turned to me, yet I felt as if I had lost a pound a second.

"Two different guns," he said. "The markings on these two bullets aren't similar in any way except in caliber."

Reaching out to pump his hand, I thanked him profusely and then explained what it was all about.

"Lucky thing for you we had that test bullet," he smiled. "Otherwise we might never have known whether he was killed by the gun you had. You could have been in quite a jam."

Thanks to Major Goddard and his blessed ballistics, I was in the clear, at least with the law. With the lawless, it was another matter.

Capone, judging from the Lingle slaying, was busy smoothing out the internal affairs of Chicago's gangland. We had refused his bribes and publicly challenged his power. I knew that when he came to "new business" we were at the top of his priority list.

Chapter 15

Buoyed by the favorable turn of events that had cleared my mind, I directed Frank to stop at a drugstore in Evanston and waited impatiently while the telephone rang in Betty's home.

Her clear, low greeting over the wire was music.

"How would you like to go to the theater tonight, starting out with dinner?"

"Are you sure you won't stand me up again?" she asked in mock anger.

"Not this time. I'm in Evanston, and if you're free tonight I'll be right over."

"Do come right over, Eliot," Betty said. "But Mother and Dad are out, so why don't we eat here and then go to the theater?"

Within a few minutes, Basile drew up in front of the roomy gabled house with its large lawn and profuse shrubbery.

"You don't have to wait," I told him. "We'll take a cab later."

The dinner was a huge success, complete with candle-light. But while we were doing the dishes, Betty's brightness vanished as she asked how the job was going.

"I wish it were all over," she said. "Eliot, it almost gives me nightmares. Dad says you well might get killed by those people. I get so I'm almost afraid to answer the telephone or pick up a newspaper for fear something may have happened to you."

"Now you run upstairs and get ready to go while I call a cab," I soothed her. "There's nothing to worry about. Why, they wouldn't think of shooting a federal man."

I hoped I was right. When she had gone upstairs, I walked out of the kitchen into the living room, fumbling for a light near the window. As I bent to switch on a lamp, I thought I saw something move in the shrubbery just outside.

My hand dropped away from the lamp, and stepping close to the wall I saw a man peering in. His figure was indistinct in the faint light from a near-by street light but the pearl gray hat stood out like a beacon.

Feeling my way cautiously, I eased out a side door lead-ing to a low veranda. My feet made no sound on the lawn as I cat-footed around the corner of the house. The shadowy figure was still there in the shrubbery, weaving stealthily from side to side in an effort to see into the various rooms.

I moved to within a few feet of him and my voice sounded loud as I snapped:

"Are you looking for me?"

He was a big man, I saw as he whirled around, and he was so startled that he gave himself away.

"No, sir, Mr. Ness."

That was proof enough for me that he was one of Capone's hoodlums, and their temerity in stalking me in Betty's home filled me with anger.

Grabbing him by the lapels of his coat, I slammed him viciously against the side of the house. As he made a motion to reach for his gun, I gave him a judo chop across the side of the neck with the flat edge of my hand. His legs buckled. I straightened him up savagely and frisked him.

He was wearing a shoulder holster, but it was empty. Obviously he had cached his gun in his automobile, preferring not to be caught armed in unfamiliar terrain.

"Listen, you ape," I said, "and get this straight. Tell whoever sent you that if I ever catch any more gorillas around here I'll put a hole in them. Not only that, but from now on there's going to be a police guard on this place. Now get out of here—and you'd better keep going."

I would have run him in, but I didn't want to upset Betty. She was alarmed enough already. As I spun him away from the house and pointed him toward the street, I couldn't resist helping him on his way with a boot that sent him sprawling some fifteen feet. He came up running and disappeared into the darkness.

Straightening my necktie, I hurried back to the veranda and quietly let myself in the side door. Betty, coming down the stairs, stopped in the hallway, and her voice held a note of sharp curiosity.

"Eliot, were you talking to someone down here? I thought I heard some sort of a commotion."

"You must be hearing things," I grinned as casually as I could. "I just caught a breath of air and almost broke my neck when I stumbled in the dark and kicked something. I'm the only one here."

I switched the conversation by calling a cab, but throughout the evening I couldn't keep my mind off that mobster at Betty's home.

"Is something bothering you?" she asked me several times. "You keep frowning to yourself every once in a while."

I ridiculed the thought, and after the theater, we had a snack at one of my favorite late restaurants. Then we walked for a while, looking into shop windows, and it was after two o'clock in the morning when I arrived home.

I was surprised to find Mother still sitting in her favorite rocking chair in the living room. But from the roundabout questions she asked, I realized that this must be a frequent vigil of worry. Everybody is worried, I thought as I went to bed. Even me, I admitted to myself—especially me.

Things looked a bit brighter the next morning when, at the office, I found an encouraging note from Robsky regarding the wire tap on the special round-the-clock telephone the syndicate had installed just to take information on our comings and goings. The note was brief:

Eliot:
The tap was a cinch. With Harrison's co-operation ran it in tonight in a couple of hours. Drafted Cloonan and Leeson to help man it. Check you later.

PAUL

With the tap in operation and everything quiet at the Montmartre wire tap, I checked over some other reports. It was a quiet day, nothing stirring, when Lahart idled into the office and said:

"Let's go out to Comiskey Park this afternoon, chief, and watch the White Sox dust off the Yankees. Ted Lyons is having a good year and he's going against Herb Pennock. It should be a good game. Besides, I need the air after experimenting with my pet project."

"Your pet project?"

Marty grinned.

"Yeah. I've been trying to discover the best wine to make a woman passionate. You might call it a lifelong project. There are an awful lot of different wines and a lot of different women."

Because it was one of those warm, sunny days when the office walls seem to close in around you, his suggestion sound fine.

"You're on," I told him.

We had lunch, with Marty rambling on about the recent heavyweight title bout between Max Schmeling and Jack Sharkey.

"Imagine that Dutchman winning on a foul," Marty shook his head sorrowfully, "and me with a five buck bet on the Boston gob. I still think Dempsey could lick both of 'em with one hand behind his back."

I had given Basile the day off, too, so we grabbed a taxi and rode out to the ball park. Out of habit, we eyed the seats around us along the first base line but close inspection satisfied us that there wasn't a single pearl gray hat in the crowd. Then we forgot all about Al Capone, breweries, bribes and bullets as we watched Lyons set the Yankees down with a meager four hits. Marty cheered lustily with boyish enthusiasm as Lyons twice struck out the mighty Babe Ruth.

162

Dropping me at my office, Marty continued on to his tour at the Montmartre wire tap.

There were no messages, and looking around for something to do I decided to attend the bouts that night at a small fight club on the West Side which was operated by a boyhood friend of mine.

Friel was waiting for me when I arrived at the office the next morning.

"What goes on, 'Blue Serge'?" I grinned at him.

He laughed at my reference to his whirl with Lahart on the speak-easy circuit and rustled several papers.

"Eliot, I can't make much out of these notes but maybe you can figure out what they mean."

Taking one of the papers, I began to skim through it.

"That call was taken by Cloonan at about three o'clock yesterday morning," Tom explained.

The notes didn't make sense, at first. Cloonan had written:
"Here's that dope for the boss."

"Okay, shoot."

"Lunch 2:00 P.M. Different spot. Office 2:30. Out car 4:00. Big hurry to G's. Out 5:30. Couple stops. Dame F.P. Shook up 'Big T.' Left together 8:10. Show. Ate new spot. Left broad off. Home 2:10 A.M. That's it. All quiet."

"Okay."

Gradually, as I read it through again, I began to get it. They had a "tail" on somebody throughout the day—and that somebody was me!

I had been followed on my trip to see Major Goddard, identified as "G." I had been checked into Betty's house in Forest Park. The hoodlum I had slapped around was evidently "Big T," probably for "Tony." And even though I drove him off, the tail had been kept on us throughout the evening.

"Let me see the other one," I directed.

"Leeson got this at one o'clock this morning," Friel said, handing it over.

This report read in the same cryptic fashion. And even though we hadn't spotted a pearl gray hat, we had had company at the ball game. The wire tap message was a complete account of my day.

"Office 8:30 A.M. Out 11:30 with 'The Laugher.' Lunch spot different again. Cab Comiskey Park. Left ball game 3:40. Mark off at Transportation Bldg. Upstairs 4:45. Out 6:00. Cab West Side restaurant. Fights. Ate again afterward. Home 12:30 A.M.

I chuckled. Marty would get a kick out of being called "The Laugher." But my humor faded as I saw that, despite our alertness, we had been tailed without knowing it. And I didn't like being the "mark." The finger apparently was on me.

The constant checkup on my comings and goings had its bright side, too. First I would have to arrange for the "Kid" to relay corroborating reports on my daily whereabouts. This might result in the mob relying enough on his information to drop the "tail" they now had following me. When that time came, I'd have them where I wanted them.

Matching wits with them was a game I would enjoy.

"Paul," I said to Robsky, "I want you and Mike King to start tailing me."

"Tailing *you?*" he asked, as if he had misunderstood.

"That's right," I smiled, "only I want you far enough back

so that you can tail the guys who are tailing me. You also better stay on your toes in case one of them gets the bright idea of rubbing me out in an impulsive moment."

We laid our plans carefully and I had a more comfortable feeling between my shoulders with the knowledge that in back of the hoods in back of me were the ever-watchful Robsky and King. Nor were they long in spotting my "tails."

"There are four of them who take turns off and on," Paul explained. "We've got them all pegged."

Next I began to feed the "Kid" a rambling casual report of where I was going and what I planned to do. For several weeks I adhered religiously to my announced schedule.

"I guess they think they've got it made," King reported not long afterward. "They've only got two tails on you now."

Eventually, as the "Kid" became more of a fixture around the office and my confidant, Robsky and King reported that I wasn't being tailed at all any longer. The "Kid" was now making the full report on my whereabouts and doings.

Meanwhile, the breweries were becoming harder to discover. The mob also knew that a raid was seldom made without my presence and apparently felt confident that the "Kid" would report daily on what I had planned for the evening.

Finally, when we uncovered another big operation on the South Side, I set them up for a surprise.

"I've a big evening planned," I said to the "Kid." "This is my parents' anniversary and I'm going to take them to the theater tonight."

But at nine o'clock that evening, when I was supposedly enjoying a show with my family, we raided one of the biggest breweries they had in operation. That haul cost them four trucks, seven men and a $200,000 plant.

The "Kid" was outraged the next day.

"How was the show?" he asked in feigned interest, bitterness creeping through his voice.

"Didn't you hear?" I grinned. "I didn't go. Something came up and I had to go water down some beer."

It wasn't funny to him. Not then, or later when I "double-crossed" the gang several more times with fake information. The "Kid" was becoming increasingly pale and jittery.

"My God, Mr. Ness," he squeaked one morning, "you're going to get us both killed. Last night Frank Nitti, the one they call 'The Enforcer,' and Bomber Belcastro, the one who makes the bombs, asked me to have a drink with them. They spent the whole time talking about how to 'take care' of people. That Belcastro said he'd like to tie a bomb to somebody's belly one time and see what would happen."

The "Kid" shuddered and wet his lips in agitation.

There was no doubt in my mind that the more raids I made on this basis, the hotter the "Kid" was becoming. The Nitti-Belcastro conversation was not too subtle a warning. Finally word sifted through to us from one of our informants that the "Kid" had "just one more chance." The stoolie was a small-time hustler named Bill Wallace whom we jokingly called "Willie, the Whisper."

"This is straight dope, Mr. Ness," said the scrawny little man with a tic in his left eye. "The way I get it, if Georgie Thomas makes one more slip—bang!"

There was nothing else to do but send the "Kid" on his long-delayed trip. When he arrived in my office, I said:

"George, how much money do you have in that Postal Savings account?"

166

"I've been saving real good, Mr. Ness," he answered. "I've got a couple thousand stashed away."

"Well," I told him, "you'd better draw it out and take a nice long trip for yourself. Time's up!"

He knew it had to come, but it caught him unprepared. Still, George Thomas wasn't one to take my words lightly. The "Kid" shook hands and disappeared from Chicago.

But he had made his point. I understand that Sandra La Flame went with him. Apparently, the "Kid" had become a big man in her bright blue eyes.

Chapter 16

It wasn't long after the "Kid" left that I came very close to getting the bullet which had my name marked on it.

My father and I were sitting in the living room talking on one of my rare evenings at home when the telephone rang in the hall and my mother answered it. She announced that it was for me.

When I answered the phone, the caller asked:

"Is this Eliot Ness?"

"Yes, it is."

I couldn't place the hoarse voice but he quickly identified himself.

"This is 'Mule' Davis."

I pictured him immediately. A pudgy, bald-headed man, Davis was a small-time bootlegger who received his nickname because of the bad hooch, or "White Mule," that he sold. We had given him a certain amount of immunity in return for secret information but I hadn't heard from him in several months.

"What's on your mind, Mule?"

"I've got to see you, Mr. Ness. It's damned important to you but I don't want to be talking over no telephones about something like this. Too many ears around. Can I come over and see you?"

I didn't like to bring my business, such as it was, into my parents' home. I worried constantly that the Capone mob might redecorate our place with a "pineapple" or send a shower of slugs through the front windows. But he sounded urgent.

"All right," I said. "How soon?"

"I'll be right over but you'll have to give me your address," he mumbled. "I been lookin' for you for a couple days but they said your folks had moved. The only way I got you finally was tryin' your old phone number."

My parents had bought a modest new home in a better neighborhood recently, but had been able to retain the old telephone number.

I gave him our new address, and just before he hung up he asked whether there was an alley behind the house. I said there was.

"I'll come up the alley and you can let me in the back door," he said.

When I returned to the living room, Mother was knitting and Dad was reading a newspaper. They both looked up expectantly, and Mother's voice was filled with trepidation.

"Is everything all right, son?"

She worried about me a great deal, fearing that I would be "killed by those murderers." Most of the time she made a brave effort to conceal her alarm but I could see her apprehension mounting almost daily in many little ways: the manner in which she watched me, the way she fussed over me and the urgent embrace she gave me—almost as if she never expected to see me alive again—every time I left the house.

Trying to allay her fears, I smiled reassuringly, kissed her on the forehead and said with all the lightness I could muster:

"Sure, Mom. Everything's all right. It's just that some fellow wants to drop by and give me some information. I'm sorry to bring him here but he insisted."

Mother shook her head.

"Characters, murderers, killers, bootleggers," she said. "I just don't know."

Dad grinned at me and then soothed her.

"Now don't worry, Mother. Eliot is big enough to take care of himself."

"Sure, Mom," I said, hoping that Dad was right. "I'll take this fellow in the kitchen when he comes."

I went into the kitchen to wait, switching off the light and turning on the one over the back porch just as a precaution. In the living room I could still hear mother scolding about "characters, murderers, killers and bootleggers."

Watching from the darkened kitchen, I soon saw Mule's dumpy figure scuttling up the alley, and as he turned into the yard I swung open the back door and called to him. Quickly he bolted inside and I flicked on the light.

"What's up, Mule?"

He wiped his forehead, slumped into a kitchen chair and let go an explosive sigh.

"Mr. Ness, I hated to bother you at home but like I said I been lookin' for you for a couple days and this I figgered you oughta know."

170

At my nod, he continued:

"Well, the pitch is this. A couple of days ago I go to a spot over in the Heights to get some corn sugar for you know what. Well, they know me there, naturally, and nobody pays me too much attention what with being around all the time.

"Well, while I'm waiting for my stuff, I drag up a chair against the wall and park myself. It's a kind of a partition made out of some kind of real thin wood or sompin' because clear as hell I can hear two guys talkin' on the other side—and who you think they're talkin' about?"

I shrugged, and he jabbed a finger in my direction.

"You, that's who. Well, when I hear 'em mention your name I sorta perk up my ears, natcherly, and I start listenin' real good, making sure meantime that there ain't nobody gonna spot me. Well, while I'm listenin' this here one guy starts tellin' the other guy that he's been picked to take care of you."

My eyes widened and "Mule" held up his right hand like a prisoner in the dock.

"Honest to God, Mr. Ness. This ain't no crap."

"Go on," I told him, "but keep your voice down so my folks don't hear you." Davis hunched over the table toward me.

"Well, as I said, I'm listenin' real close now and this one guy says to the other one, real businesslike: 'Mike, the boss says that you're to do this as soon as possible.' Then the other guy says: 'I'll take care of it.' So then the other guy says to him: 'You're to use the bullets with the cross on the nose so the hole will be big enough to make sure that it's a good job.' And the last thing I hear is the other guy saying, 'It will be done.' "

171

"Mule" wiped his forehead again, like a man finishing a hard day's work.

"Well," he went on, "I got away from that wall real quiet like and moved over to the far end of the room. Good thing, too. Cuz in about a minute they come around the back of that partition and walk out of the joint. All I can tell you is that one was a fat greaseball and the other one was a tough-lookin' little geezer who looked like he might use a stiletto on you and clean his fingernails with it fifteen minutes later."

I was surprised that I didn't feel too perturbed about learning that I was marked for gangland execution. Probably underneath, I mused, I had been expecting just this for a long time.

"Anything else?" I asked him.

"Nothing that I can think of," Davis frowned in concentration. "But I sure wanted you to know about it because you been real nice to some of us little guys, what with one thing and another."

"I can't thank you enough, 'Mule,'" I said as he rose nervously, anxious to be on his way.

"Okay, okay," he replied, and then he was gone into the night.

After he left, I sat there for some time trying to figure out what to do. Certainly I couldn't stay in my parents' home, because I didn't want any trigger-happy gangster putting a stake-out on me around here. And I would also have to make certain that they were protected.

"Did you get your business all taken care of?" Mother asked as I walked back into the living room.

"In a manner of speaking," I smiled at her. "There's just one thing, Mom, and I don't want you worrying about it.

We've received a hot tip on something I have to follow up, and I won't be home for a few days. I'll call you and let you know how things are going."

Dad looked at me shrewdly. His voice was gruff, but proud.

"Take good care of yourself, son."

That night I packed enough clothes to last me for some time. When Basile came early the next morning to pick me up, we drove to the district police station and I arranged with the captain in charge to put a twenty-four-hour guard on my parents' home.

"Now we'll go to the office," I told Basile, "and please try not to let the car be stolen today because my clothes will be in it."

Once there, I summoned Lahart and Robsky and gave them a complete report on what "Mule" Davis had told me.

"What I've got in mind," I explained, "is to get a room someplace until I can nail the gunman who's looking for me. Naturally, I'm a bit partial to this hide of mine, so I'm going to need your help until I do."

They nodded agreement and I said:

"Marty, four eyes are better than two, so we'll have to work as a team until I can find this gent."

"Suits me fine, chief," he acknowledged. "It might be interesting before it's over."

Turning to Robsky, I said:

"Paul, I want to be certain that nobody tails us while I'm finding a room. I don't mind watching for them all day but I sure like to sleep without having a guard outside my door."

I directed Robsky to tail us while we rode around the city for about an hour. Then, when he was certain that we weren't being followed, he could signal us and I would drive to the rooming house where I planned to stay.

Robsky left to "lose" himself outside before taking up a position from which to follow us and, an hour later, Marty and I went down to the car which Basile had ready. Both of us were watchful as we drove away, and it was quite a while before I could even spot Robsky in our wake.

We drove aimlessly through sections where there was little traffic so that a "tail" would soon be detected. Finally, Robsky sped past with a wave of his hand and parked a block ahead of us until we were well ahead, taking up the trail again when we were almost out of sight.

Satisfied that we were not being followed, I had Frank drive to the rooming house I had selected and rented an inside third-floor bedroom looking out on a blind court. The door was stout, and as long as I made certain that I wasn't being tailed before I came home, I was reasonably certain that my nights would be restful.

For the next three days Marty was at my side constantly during the daytime, with Robsky inconspicuously bringing up the rear.

All we knew about the killer on my trail was that his name was Mike. Not much to go on. But finally Basile came up with the information we needed.

Frank had a friend known as the "Clown," a grotesque hanger-on in the fringes of gangdom, who was neither intelligent enough to be a gangster nor honest enough to be a workman. Seeking him out, Basile learned that the man looking for me was a Maffia gunman whose last name was Picchi.

Working swiftly, I obtained a rogues gallery photograph

of him. The picture showed a stringy, gaunt-cheeked man with hooded eyes and slicked-down hair.

Now that I knew the man I was looking for, I went out to find him before he could find me.

He seemed to be taking his time because during the two succeeding days there was no indication of anyone following me. But on the third day, as we made easy bait of ourselves by driving slowly through Chicago Heights, Frank spoke tensely without turning his head:

"Boss, I'm pretty sure we got a car on our tail."

Warning Marty not to look back, I gave Frank directions.

"Keep your eye on it in the rear-view mirror and make a few turns so we can be sure it's following us. Meanwhile, hit a red light so that it will get a bit closer and maybe you can see how many there are in the car."

Basile cruised back and forth and finally caught a long stop by halting for a traffic signal just as it began to turn red.

"It's slowed down to a walk, but now it's close enough so I can see there's only one guy in it," Frank advised us. He delayed as the light changed and then, shifting into gear, said: "Boss, I'm sure it's the guy in the picture."

"Fine," I told him. "Now up ahead about ten blocks there's a real narrow street with high buildings on each side running right up to the corner. About three blocks from there, take off like a bat out of Hell, swing left into that street and about fifty yards after you make the turn stop as quickly as you can and pull the car diagonally across the street so he can't get past."

What I had in mind was that Picchi would be around

that corner and in behind our blockade before he could see
us and swerve back to the open street we were on now.

"Here we go, boss," Basile said.

The car lurched forward and Frank announced:

"He's coming right along."

"Good," I replied, and turning to Lahart I ordered: "After
we hit that corner and Frank starts to slow down, get back
and nail this guy."

We were really rolling when our car reached the designated corner. The tires squealed as Frank gunned it into the
turn and then, straightening out, he slammed on the brakes.
The car slued across the street, and I knew Picchi couldn't
get past as I flung open the door and raced back toward the
corner with Marty at my heels. We had taken only a few
steps when the car following us careened around the corner
and skidded to a halt with one wheel up on the sidewalk.

At the wheel was the little cobra-eyed man in the picture.
I raced up to the driver's door and yanked it open. Eyes glittering, Picchi's hand darted under his coat and withdrew
a revolver.

But I had my gun out and smashed it savagely down on
his gun hand just below the wrist. The pistol fell to the floor
of the car, and the old hot anger welled up in me as I reached
in, grabbed his coat collar and dragged him out of the car.
He came out kicking, and after giving him enough room to
stand up I brought my fist crashing down on top of his
head. He went down.

Marty covered him as I reached into the car and retrieved
his revolver.

It was a killer's gun. The mob's method was to shoot the
victim and leave the gun, with the serial numbers filed off,

next to the body. The numbers were gone from this one.

Flipping open the cylinder, I saw the final proof. The man who had been sent to get me had been ordered to use bullets "with the cross on the nose so that the hole will be big enough." Each of the bullets that fell into the palm of my hand had a deep cross cut across the soft lead nose.

"Dumdum" bullets—and meant for me.

They felt cold as I cradled them in my fist. I decided that they were going to be fired on the target range—and I intended to keep one as a reminder of how we had to make our own luck.

Loading Picchi into our car, I kept him covered while Frank drove us to the Kensington Police Station. Marty followed along behind in the killer's car. Once there, we had him held overnight, to be booked before the United States Commissioner the following morning.

As we drove away, I fingered the dumdum bullets in my pocket and took the first easy breath I had drawn in several days. This might afford us only a brief respite, I realized, but at least it was a welcome lull. Yet, even so, I couldn't erase from my mind the thought that Capone and the Maffia would not be beaten so easily.

They had plenty of other killers at their command.

CHAPTER 17

That the removal of one gunman from circulation had not thwarted the designs of Al Capone and the Maffia was driven home to me the very next afternoon.

I was sitting in the office, going over some reports, when the telephone rang.

"Ness speaking," I said into the mouthpiece.

The voice I heard was flat, cold and menacing.

"Listen, big shot, I've got a few words for you."

"Who is this?" I asked.

"Never mind. I got a message for you. You've had your last chance to be smart. Just keep it in mind that sometime soon you're going to be found lying in a ditch with a hole in your head and your wang slashed off. We'll just keep reminding you so you won't forget to remember."

The line went dead.

What I had been promised was the favorite demise of the Maffia killers. They took their victim for a one-way ride, blew out his brains, hacked off the genital organs with a stiletto and cast them scornfully beside the body.

Ordinary human beings found the savage ways of the Maffia not only difficult but almost impossible to believe. Yet, from the sketchy details supplied by informers such as "Willie, the Whisper," and "The Clown," together with what we were able to pry from frightened witnesses hoping for a "break" or some sort of leniency, we were only too familiar with their methods of extermination.

Most of those we arrested or interrogated wouldn't say a word, true to the code of Omerta, the law of silence enforced by quick assassination for those who broke it. Others refused to speak out of a warped sense of loyalty. They had been well bought, those like the pear-shaped bail bondsman who admitted freely and openly that he was a friend of Capone's "and the hell with them that don't like it."

"I've got twenty-five tailor-made suits and fifty pairs of handmade shoes," he boasted. "See this necktie? Twenty bucks a copy. Well, y'wanta know somethin'? When I was a ragged-assed kid, standing on a corner peddlin' newspapers, a guy comes along and gives me a fifty-dollar bill for a paper. I says to him, 'Jeez, mister, I ain't got change for this.'

"So this guy turns to me and says, 'Who the hell asked ya for change.' You know who that guy was? Well, it was Al Capone. And he bought me, right then and there. Not only that, I been workin' for him ever since and, as I say, I didn't never know things could be so good."

Yet there are always those who "talk" out of fear, hatred, friendship or greed. From them, and other sources, we had been able gradually to piece together the sordid and violent story of the Maffia in Chicago.

The Maffia, or Black Hand Society, was brought to America by Ignazio Saietta, known as "Lupo, the Wolf," in 1899. Open only to Sicilians, it required a slashed-wrist to slashed-wrist initiation rite as a token of unbreakable blood brotherhood.

At the time when Johnny Torrio took over from "Diamond Jim" Colosimo and raised young Al Capone to the status of a partner, the Maffia was not all-powerful in Chicago and had not yet begun to dream of becoming the nation-wide syndicate into which it later developed. Mike Merlo, head of the Unione Siciliano, was hardly dead when the national chieftain Frankie Uale, also known as Frankie Yale, and the Torrio-Capone combination sought control of Chicago in a bloody battle with Joe Aiello.

Capone, because he was of Neapolitan descent, was ineligible to become president of the Chicago Maffia. Torrio could be—and sought it. So, too, did Aiello, who was allied with the "Bugs" Moran gang, sworn enemies of Torrio and Capone.

Torrio, however, had long been a friend of Uale and therefore received the coveted appointment. Brooklyn Johnny didn't last long. The Moran gang chased him up Michigan Avenue with blazing guns and Torrio, recovering from his wounds, gave up his territory to Capone and abdicated as leader of the Maffia.

Capone nominated Tony Lombardo, one of his mob, for the "vacancy," but Uale, fearing more trouble from the Aiello-Moran gang, hesitated to take sides. Capone visited Uale in New York and was directed to go home and make peace "for the good of the Unione." Capone went back to Chicago and then protested vigorously to Uale that he had uncovered a machine gun nest overlooking the cigar store where he met often with Lombardo.

Uale saw through what was apparently a plot to kill Lombardo. The crafty Capone had engineered it himself to discredit Aiello!

"For the last time, does Lombardo get the job?" Capone asked Uale through an emissary.

Frankie Uale refused to make a choice.

Shortly afterward, on a summer day in 1928, an automobile bearing Illinois license plates drove up alongside Uale's car on a Brooklyn street. A machine gun chattered and Frankie Uale died as his car leaped the curb and crashed into a house.

Torrio, back in Brooklyn, stepped in as national chief of the Maffia. Lombardo, quite naturally, got the top job in Chicago.

But again the Unione throne in the Windy City was a chair of death.

Lombardo, a quiet man with a fine home in Cicero, ostensibly ran a wholesale grocery house which had a tremendous trade among Italian storekeepers and restaurateurs. It was healthier for them that way. He also handled tremendous amounts of sugar which was peddled to bootleg distilleries.

Just a little more than two months after he had assumed his new role as Capone's puppet, Lombardo made his daily visit to the Italo-American National Union in the Hartford Building at Dearborn and Madison streets. Late in the afternoon, at the height of the home-going rush, he left the building with two of his bodyguards.

They were in the heart of the business district, surrounded by hundreds of unsuspecting citizens and only one block east of the intersection of State and Madison streets, one of the world's busiest corners.

Yet even there, gangland guns dared to defy law and order. Shots rang out and Lombardo lay dead on the sidewalk. There were two gaping holes in his head, the silver dollar size made only by the dumdum bullet—the kind of holes I had escaped by getting to Picchi before he could get to me.

Capone was undaunted by Lombardo's sudden demise. He immediately installed Pasqualino "Patsy" Lolordo in the bloody chair.

Patsy lived on the third floor of a ramshackle tenement, but his apartment was furnished luxuriously. One afternoon, early in 1929, three men knocked at the door and Patsy greeted them jovially. Patsy called his wife, who was ironing in the kitchen, to bring some wine. For an hour they drank and laughed. Then came the crash of shots and Patsy died with eleven bullet holes in him. As Mrs. Lolordo rushed into the room she saw one of the men, a smoking pistol in his hand, gently ease a pillow under Patsy's head to make his last moments more comfortable.

Mrs. Lolordo positively identified a rogues' gallery photograph of Joseph Aiello as one of the murderers. But no Sicilian breaks Omerta. She later denied the identification.

Aiello now planned a master stroke to get rid of Capone. Two of the most deadly Maffia killers were John Scalise and Albert Anselmi. They had done much extermination work for Capone, but Aiello wooed them carefully.

Joe Guinta, known as "the dancing man," had recently appeared in Chicago "from the East." Aiello picked him as a candidate for the vacant Maffia leadership, and on the promise of great rewards he induced Capone's friends Scalise and Anselmi to convince "Scarface Al" that Guinta was the best man for the empty throne. Capone consented.

But before the coronation, "Scarface Al" wanted to know more about Guinta. His espionage system soon reported that Guinta had been seen in conference at a North Side restaurant with Scalise, Anselmi and his deadly enemy Aiello.

Capone didn't cancel the coronation.

The unsuspecting trio of plotters—Aiello, of course, not being invited—were in high spirits at the celebration party at Burnham one night in May of 1929. The cabaret was jammed with Capone mobsters; Guinta, Scalise and Anselmi were placed in the seats of honor at a sumptuous banquet table.

Champagne corks popped. Huge plates of chicken and spaghetti were consumed. Capone smiled broadly at them and finally, the feast over and the tables cleared, Capone rose and offered a toast.

"To the guests of honor."

Then the smile vanished from his face. Fury blazed in his eyes.

"Guests of honor," he roared. "Traitors! Double-crossers!"

Guinta, Scalise and Anselmi were rooted to their chairs. They turned white and trembled violently. Their deception was known! Powerless under the guns of Capone's bodyguards, they sat there as Capone screamed:

"Get the bats! Whoever crosses Capone gets his!"

A number of heavy baseball bats were produced. Capone grabbed one in his meaty hands and his short, powerful arms swept up and down. Scalise toppled with a crushed skull. Again and again he raised the bat and swung it down, first on Guinta and then on Anselmi. Others joined in then, and pistols finished the job.

The next day the three crushed and riddled bodies were found in a ditch near Hammond, Indiana.

Guinta had been crowned—with a baseball bat.

The horrified Aiello knew that such double-dealing as he had inspired could not go unpunished. Desperate, he offered a reward of fifty thousand dollars to the man who would rub out Al Capone. There were no takers.

For more than a year, Aiello dodged the ready bullets. Finally he decided to get out, and while waiting his chance he went into hiding in a quiet residential district on the far West Side. No one, he was sure, knew where he was, and he had obtained tickets for Brownsville, Texas, with the idea of getting across the border and disappearing.

Finally, on the night of October 30, 1930, he made his move. Allowing just enough time to make his train, he called a taxicab and sprinted for it.

Aiello never made it.

The man who had believed himself safely hidden was greeted by a hail of lead from a machine gun in a second-floor apartment across the street. And when he swerved back toward the protection of the building from which he just had come, another machine gun on the third floor of that very building blazed in his face. He was dead before he hit the ground, fifty-nine bullet holes making a sieve of his body.

Aiello had been hiding in that apartment house for two weeks, supposedly unknown. The machine guns had been waiting for him exactly thirteen days!

As the chatter of the machine guns stilled and Aiello's ambition drained from his body with his blood, five men dashed from the apartments and disappeared into the night. It was written off by the police as an unsolved crime.

Yet this, whispered our informers, was only one in the long line of Capone slayings.

At long last, the Maffia in Chicago was Capone's completely. The Sicilian killers finally were his alone to command. The Unione Siciliano was his tool!

This was what we opposed with our pitiful handful of men. We had chosen to battle them in what now shaped up as a war to the finish. And every day, for an entire week, they reminded me that they were watching and waiting.

The daily pattern was always the same.

The telephone would ring, and a voice with a faint trace of a foreign accent would have me grinding my teeth impotently.

"Hello, big shot. How does it feel to be waiting to get it? It won't be long now."

Then the line would go dead.

At first I tried to ignore it. But when it happened for the fifth day in a row, it began to rasp on my nerves.

Finally, on the sixth day, I began to taunt him, interrupting after the usual greeting of "Hello, big shot."

"What's the matter with you punks?" I laughed into the receiver. "Can't you find any old ladies to rob or any kids to scare?"

The voice lost its flat calmness and hissed a string of swear words.

This time I hung up.

I was primed the next day. The caller, whoever he was, hadn't finished his usual greeting when I interrupted.

"You grave robbers haven't got the guts to shoot anybody who's looking."

Again I hung up.

There were no more calls.

But now I was more watchful than ever. Again I had Lahart with me wherever I went and either Robsky or King as my protective "tail" to check on whether anybody was following us.

At night I always went home to my rented room by devious routes, entering strange office buildings, taking the elevator up to a floor I chose at random, and walking down the back exits. I used every dodge I'd ever heard of and finally went so far as to stay at a different hotel each night. I just couldn't help remembering Aiello and the machine gun nests that had been so swiftly planted around his "secret" hide-out.

During this period I wouldn't allow myself to see Betty. As long as there was any threat hanging over me, I couldn't permit myself to endanger her, no matter how badly I wanted to be with her. Nor would I visit my parents. I had to content myself with frequent telephone calls.

Betty, in particular, sounded worried when I called her one afternoon and evaded another date.

"I stopped by to see your mother and she told me that you were on some sort of a lead and hadn't been home for some time. Is everything all right, Eliot?"

I made my voice as casual as possible.

"Everything's just fine, honey. How are you, and how are Mother and Dad?"

"We're all fine," she said. "You know, of course, that there's a police guard on your house—and on ours, too. Well, I actually think your mother is enjoying it. When I got there, she had two detectives sitting in the kitchen eating freshly baked cake and drinking coffee. She told me they were good company and one of them told me that it was the best duty he ever had."

We talked a while longer, and then Betty demanded in a firm tone:

"Are you sure everything is all right and that you're not in danger?"

I told her not to be silly.

"It's just that we're working on something that I can't talk about right now, particularly on the telephone. But I'll have it worked out in a few days."

How casual can you get, I wondered grimly after we had said our reluctant good-byes. Well, they had run me out of my home but I'd be damned if they'd run me out of Chicago.

It stood to reason that something had to break soon, yet I was determined that it wasn't going to be Eliot Ness.

It almost was—that very evening.

We had left our building and were in the middle of the block, Marty beside me and King covering us at some distance behind, when I suggested to Lahart that we go to a restaurant across the street and have a cup of coffee. Marty agreed, and I left him behind a few feet as I veered between two cars parked at the curb and started out across the street.

I heard the high-pitched whine of the powerful motor at the same moment Marty yelled hoarsely:

"Eliot! Look out!"

Without thinking, I spun and dove headlong back between the two parked cars. My chest crashed against the curb, driving the breath from my body, as the roaring machine rushed by inches from my drawn-in legs. By the time

I dragged myself painfully to my feet, the speeding car was out of sight around the next corner.

Marty's face was chalk white as he came around the car while King pounded up to us.

"Jeez-us but that was close!"

"Did you get a look at them?" I gasped, struggling for breath.

"Two guys—but I couldn't recognize them," he said. "But you wanting a cup of coffee probably saved our bacon. One guy had a Tommy-gun and I'll bet next week's pay check they were going to gun us down. But when they saw you start out in the street they decided to run you down—and when they missed they were going so fast and so close that the guy didn't have time to use the chopper."

Marty's face was still white and King had his lower lip between his teeth. Looking down at my suit, I knew I was more shaken than either of them. The war was on.

CHAPTER 18

A few days later, the storm broke. Arriving at the office even earlier than usual to go over some reports, I was hard at work and hadn't noticed the passage of time until Lahart walked in and asked if I was ready to go to lunch.

Looking at my watch, I saw that it was after eleven o'clock and I suggested a restaurant on Michigan Boulevard.

"Tell Basile to bring the car around," I said, "while I just finish going over this last report."

"He wasn't there when I came in but I'll look again," Marty replied.

Going to the door, he scanned the outer office and called over his shoulder: "Frank's not here."

"That's peculiar," I remarked. "Now that you mention it, I haven't seen him all morning."

Disturbed, I reached for the telephone and called his home. His wife Enis answered almost immediately.

"Frank?" she asked.

"No, this is Eliot Ness. Is Frank there?"

189

Worry tinged her voice as she answered.

"No, he isn't, Mr. Ness. He hasn't been home all night. I thought probably he was out with you somewhere. Don't you know where he is?"

"Now don't get upset," I told her. "He's probably around checking up on something. I'll get in touch with him and have him call you as soon as I contact him."

"Please do," she said with a trace of panic.

I comforted her, rather lamely.

"Everything will be all right. Don't worry."

But I did. It wasn't like Basile to disappear without a word. A pencil snapped between my fingers as I put in a call to Detective Captain William H. Schoemaker, one of Chicago's honest cops.

After what seemed like ages, I heard his strong, sure voice on the other end.

"Captain Schoemaker speaking."

"Shoes," I said, "this is Eliot Ness."

"Greetings, Eliot. How are things in the liquor business?"

"Fine," I said. "How are they with you?"

He chuckled.

"Not too good. I must be getting old. I hit a hoodlum this morning and he didn't stay down."

I grinned at what was probably the truth, although I would have laid a bet that the old fire eater's opponent didn't get up.

"Shoes," I explained, "my chauffeur Frank Basile didn't show up today and his wife tells me he wasn't home last night. Things have been getting a little hot around here and I wondered whether you'd check around and see if you can get any word on him."

"I'll see what I can find out," he promised briskly and rang off.

Next I called the garage and was informed that Basile hadn't been in to pick up the car. Now I was getting really worried. Marty and I waited by the telephone for Captain Schoemaker to call back.

Shortly after noon, the phone rang. It was the captain and he sounded concerned.

"Eliot, I may have some bad news for you. But don't get all heated up because this may not be your man."

My knuckles showed white on the telephone as I waited.

"Anyhow," Schoemaker added, "I contacted the state police and they were in the process of filing a report. They found a body in a ditch outside Chicago Heights just a little while ago. It was pretty well shot up and there wasn't any identification. They thought probably it was just another mobster taken for a ride."

"Where's the body now, Shoes?"

"They took it over to Doty's Funeral Home next to the Kensington Police Station. But don't get steamed up until you go over and take a look at it because it may not be your man."

"Thanks, Shoes," I told him heavily. "I hope it isn't but, well, I've got a terrible feeling."

Still hoping against hope, I related the details to Lahart. His usually laughing eyes narrowed and there was a white, pinched look around his mouth.

"Let's go," he said sharply.

The ride to the South Side was one of the longest of my life, although Marty drove with reckless urgency. We pulled up in front of Doty's Funeral Home, and looking at the

191

neat brick building with the wide glass window in the front, I had to steel myself to make the journey up the flower-bordered walk leading to the white door.

Fear had a relentless grip on my throat, making it difficult to breathe. From the depths of the quiet flower-scented rooms inside, I heard a melodious chime in answer to the jab of my finger on the button. The wait seemed interminable before the door swung open and we were facing a bland, unctuous man peering birdlike through a pince-nez from which trailed a black ribbon that looped around his neck.

"Yes, gentlemen?"

"We're from the United States District Attorney's office," I said, flipping out my credentials. "I understand the state police brought a body here a little while ago that was found out in the Heights. We'd like to take a look at it."

"Oh, yes," he nodded, dropping his welcome-customer look. "You mean the unfortunate gentleman who had the, er, accident."

"That's the one," I told him.

"Follow me, please."

Standing aside to usher us in, he shut the door with the typical gentleness of his trade, and the musty odor of weeping flowers closed in around us. I had always flinched at the smell of these places and I breathed shallowly as he led us along a thickly carpeted hallway and through the rear into a bare, chilly room in which the only furnishings were two white enameled surgical cabinets such as you see in hospitals, a straight-backed white metal chair, and a large enameled waste bucket with a foot-pedal top.

There also were two flat, rubber-wheeled carts which hospitals use for stretcher patients.

Both of them were occupied, their rigid mounds draped with white rubber sheets.

I moved toward one of them, barely conscious that Marty was alongside me, and the mortician leaned over and drew back the sheet. A gusty breath rushed from my throat. It wasn't Basile but a grizzled ancient with hollow cheeks and a marble, vein-studded forehead.

My relief was short duration.

"Sorry, gentlemen," the mortician intoned regretfully, his voice filled with self-reproach. "This is not the one. This gentleman was, ah, quite natural."

We turned to walk across the room to the other slab. My throat tightened when he reached down to draw back the sheet, and as the rubber peeled away I felt hot tears stinging the corner of my eyes, a roaring in my ears.

Lying there was a lifeless husk which had been Frank Basile!

I had expected it, I suppose, and in the course of my career I had often witnessed the ravages of violent death. You think, eventually, that nothing can disturb you and that your nerves are impregnable. Yet, looking down at that familiar face, different somehow in its final repose, I realized that death is something to which we never become calloused if the person is someone close.

I had seen gangsters who could cut out your heart with a dull butter knife and enjoy it become soft as putty while holding their children close. The murderous Dion O'Bannion would turn doe eyed while working with flowers in his own shop.

Never before had I been unable to understand the emotions of such men. Yet now, somehow, I thought that I did.

193

Everyone had his Achilles' heel. No one was as completely calloused as he thought.

I stood there, eyes riveted on the strong, bold face. And my stare was drawn irresistibly to the gaping hole just above the left ear.

"Dumdum," I breathed.

Marty's voice was a growl and his hand closed on my arm like a steel band.

"Bastards!"

Carefully, I drew the clammy rubber sheet up over the immobile face and thought of how much I owed this big man lying there on a slab meant for me.

Again I remembered that night in Pete Scalonas' saloon when the killer in the candy-striped silk shirt stood behind me with a poised stiletto and Frank's muttered warning saved my life. Once more I saw his big hands on the wheel of our steel-bumpered truck as he drove it through brewery doors, and recalled his readiness to stand beside me throughout my days as a clay pigeon, undaunted by the imminent prospect of a sudden hail of lead.

"So help me God," I vowed, "I'll see that whoever did this pays with his life."

I dreaded the thought of telling his wife. But it had to be done, and Mrs. Basile, a handsome woman with haunted eyes, appeared to have expected the worst and took it stonily.

"I know he was not afraid," she whispered, quivering lips betraying the dryness of her eyes. "He was a good man. What else can anyone say?"

What else, indeed, I thought as we drove away, and then my mind hardened as I abandoned everything else to set out on the trail of the killer.

"Let's find the 'Clown.' " I told Marty. "If anybody knows anything, or can find out anything about this, he's the one."

We drove to the Heights, each busy with his own thoughts and memories, and began to search the haunts of the man known as "Clown." Eventually we traced him to a grubby little room in the basement of a tenement apartment, the odors of a near-by stable seeping in through two tiny windows high in one wall looking out on an alley stacked with broken boxes and barrels.

The naked bulb in a brassy wall fixture lit up a battered couch covered with a dirty patchwork quilt. Leaning drunkenly against one of the aged plaster walls was a soiled bureau with a cracked mirror. A mongrel pup curled in a cardboard carton beside the couch; newspapers were stacked high in one shadowy corner and the uncoiled wire of a lifeless spring drooped listlessly from the split seat of a worn overstuffed chair.

"Y'll hafta sit on the couch, I guess," the Clown mumbled as we pushed inside.

"We'll stand," I told him. "What we want to know won't take very long."

The "Clown" shifted from one foot to the other and slumped on the creaking couch, one gnarled hand dropping to the pup's head.

"Did you hear about Frank Basile?" I demanded.

"Yeah, I heard." The tremulous voice was listless.

"Well, what do you know about it?"

The "Clown's" grotesque head came up and I was surprised to see a tear slide down one misshapen cheek. Again I knew wonder. Here was a miserable, poverty-stricken wretch barely existing in one of society's sewers, yet he cherished a forlorn stray and wept over another's death.

"I know somethin', all right," he snuffled. "An' I'll be glad t'tell ya. That Basile, he was my friend. He never laughed at me cuz I was ugly—or pushed me around. He'd even buy me a drink and sit with me. He was my friend, Frank was. Sure I'll tell you somethin'."

Defiance gleamed in his rheumy eyes as he picked up the pup to cradle it against the front of a greasy leather jacket.

"Yesterday I'm walkin' past Pete's poolroom, y'know, the one where the Unione meets. So I looks in the window and I sees three or four guys kissin' each other."

Hesitating, he glanced up from the pup and asked:

"Y'know what that means, Mr. Ness?"

"Yes," I nodded, the "kiss of death!"

That expression later was to lose its original meaning through popular usage. But it evolved from the fact that when a Maffia killer was selected, by tradition he was given a ceremonial "kiss of death" by all those at the conclave.

"That's right," he continued. "When they pick somebody to knock somebody off, they always go through that rigmarole. Well, right off I figure some bird has had it. But natcherly I don't know who."

His voice softened regretfully as he added: "I wished to Jesus I had."

Interrupting, I prodded:

"Did you see the man they were kissing?"

The "Clown's" gargoyle head bobbed up and down.

"Yeah. It was a guy they call Tony Napoli."

"Thanks very much," I said. "You've helped us a lot."

"Glad to do it, Mr. Ness. I hope ya git the bastard and

I hope he fries. Frank was my friend. He never treated me like those other guys."

The "Clown" was still blubbering, straining the pup to his chest, as we let ourselves out of the odorous room and climbed the filthy concrete steps into the clean air outside.

"Do you know this guy?" Marty asked.

I shook my head, wishing that I did.

"We'll have to go see Captain Mike Grady at the Kensington station and find out whether he does."

When we were closeted with Grady, I told him what we knew and Grady said:

"That's one of about half a dozen names he uses, but I know the guy. He's a hatchet-faced dude who we've known for a long time has been associated with the Maffia. I'll put out a pickup order on him."

"We'd sure like to help," I told him.

"Well, now, Eliot," he grinned at me sympathetically, "I know how you must feel. But I've got a hunch that if you went after him and caught him he'd never make it to the station. You'd better let us get him unless, of course, you do happen to run into him first."

We tried. Leaving the police station, Marty and I began to backtrack Basile's movements of the previous night. From various sources we learned that he had played cards with friends and started home not long after midnight. Somewhere he had been intercepted and taken on "the big trip."

Shortly before noon the next day, my phone rang, and when I answered I heard Captain Grady's voice.

"We've got your man, Eliot, but he has an alibi. He claims he spent the whole night with some skirt named Maybelle Waters on the South Side—and she backs him up."

197

"Give me her address," I barked. "I want to talk to her."

Jotting it down, I called Marty and we drove to the place, a broken-down apartment house. We found Maybelle Waters in her cold-water flat. She was a short, big-busted woman in her early thirties, nursing a black eye.

We didn't waste any time with her.

"Listen, beautiful," Marty cracked, "we happen to know that Tony Napoli wasn't here last night. So you'd better talk—and fast."

"That's right," I said. "You don't want to get into trouble, do you?"

Pointing to her eye, she shrilled:

"You guys want me to get more of this?"

"No," I told her. "And we'll make sure nobody bothers you. But why should you alibi for a guy who's keeping another woman, too?"

She tried to feign disbelief, but her eyes glittered.

"I thought that lousy bastard was two-timin' me. Okay. So he wasn't here until five o'clock this mornin'. Then he beat on me and left, so t'hell with him."

"Will you sign a statement to that effect?" I asked.

"Y'r damned right," she snapped. "I'm gonna git t'hell out of this crummy town anyhow."

"Fine, now you're being sensible and keeping yourself out of trouble," I said. "Now get ready and we'll go down to the station."

But we were too late.

When we arrived at the station, Captain Grady had left orders for us to come to his office if we showed up.

"I've been trying to reach you," he said. "What do you

198

think happened? Napoli hanged himself in his cell with his necktie."

Omerta, the deadly law of silence, had been kept again.

"It's all right with me," I told Grady. "Somehow or other he just might have beaten this rap."

This way I was satisfied. Basile's murder was avenged, his killer dead.

Yet it wasn't very comforting. For us it was a bad trade. They had plenty of killers left. Enough to go all the way around, as far as we were concerned, and they callously could afford a one-for-one trade. We couldn't. And each of us wondered who was ticketed for the next "one-way ride."

CHAPTER 19

Although Basile had been avenged, I was more determined than ever to show Capone that the ruthless murder he ordered only served to increase the defiance of "The Untouchables."

My chance came very soon.

Not long after Frank's funeral, I received notification that the government's contract was expiring on the garage in which our fleet of confiscated trucks was stored. The contract had been bid in by another garage on the other side of town.

We had, by now, a tremendous collection of rolling stock. All told, there were forty-five trucks which would later be sold at public auction.

They were all shapes and all sizes, from half-ton pickup trucks to ten-ton vans and glass-lined tank trucks. Most of them were new, or nearly so, and moving them would require only a small crew to drive them to the new garage in shifts.

But seething inside with a desire to show "Scarface Al" that we were unintimidated, I evolved a brilliant psychological counterstroke.

Why not move them all at once, in a tremendous convoy, and drive the entire lot straight past the Lexington Hotel headquarters of the flabby-faced gang overlord?

Delighted with the thought, I called Lahart in and laid the plan before him. He grinned appreciatively.

"A helluva fine idea," he enthused. "But wouldn't it be a shame if he missed the show?"

"I can take care of that, too," I snickered. "Damned if I won't call up the Lexington and tip them off that something big is going to happen right out front."

Plotting like two schoolboys, we began to make our plans.

"It'll take a couple of days to line up that many drivers," Marty said. "But you leave it to me, chief. I'll find 'em if I have to teach 'em to drive myself."

I proceeded to fill in our whole crew on the plan.

"Just one thing," I warned over their delighted grins. "We've got to be certain that we don't get hijacked. So in addition to the fleet of trucks, we'll put two men to a car and give the fleet a mobile, well-armed convoy. If they want trouble, we'll give it to them in spades."

"I hope they try," grunted Seager, summing it up for the whole group.

Two days before we were scheduled to move the fleet, Marty and I drove to the garage where I issued orders that every truck was to be cleaned up.

"I want those big, expensive tank trucks to really gleam," I told one of the attendants.

When we gathered at the garage on the morning of the

transfer, I was pleased to see that my orders had been carried out to the letter. The newer trucks glittered and I knew it would be an impressive motorcade.

Marty's drivers were checked in and assigned to their trucks and then we laid out the route we would follow. It was a circuitous drive because, actually, we had no reason to go anywhere near the Lexington. But I intended to take those trucks right up Michigan Avenue before we swung back toward the new garage.

Gathering my men, I gave them final instructions.

"Marty and I will ride in the lead car," I explained. "Right behind us will come Chapman and Gardner. Then count off fifteen trucks before Robsky and Cloonan slip into line. After the next fifteen trucks, Friel and King get in the parade, and after the last fifteen trucks, the rear is to be brought up by Seager and Leeson."

That gave me a protection car in between each group of fifteen trucks, which was spreading it a bit thin, but there was no other way to handle it.

The reason I wanted two cars at the front was so that when we came to the Lexington Marty and I could pull up right in front of the hotel until the whole procession had passed. Chapman and Gardner could take over the lead at that point and head our motorcade to the new garage.

In this manner, Marty and I could keep watchful eyes on the Lexington in case there was any general movement among the gangsters to head for their cars and attempt to intercept us.

They nodded their understanding and all of us hefted sawed-off shotguns. Any would-be hijackers were in for a battle.

"Just one thing before we take off," I laughed with a
wink. "I have to make a telephone call."

Their laughter followed me as I walked into the garage
office, a tiny room cluttered with spare parts, and asked the
attendant sitting at a scarred roll-top desk whether he would
mind stepping outside while I made a personal telephone
call.

"Not at all, Mr. Ness," he assured me.

I put in my call. The girl at the switchboard answered in
affected tones.

"Put me through to Mr. Capone," I directed.

"Just a moment, please."

I could hear the buzzing sound which indicated she was
ringing the Capone offices upstairs, and then a heavy voice
answered.

"Yeah?"

"Let me talk to 'Snorkey,'" I growled authoritatively,
using as an open sesame the nickname allowed only to his
intimates.

"Who's callin'?" the voice demanded.

"None of your God-damned business," I snarled. "But if
you know what's good for you, you'll put him on here
damned quick."

The voice took on an apologetic air.

"Keep your shirt on. I'll see if he's here."

There was a pause and then a smooth, cold voice came
over the wire.

"Who's this?" I asked.

The reply was impatient.

"Capone."

"Well, Snorkey," I said, "I just wanted to tell you that if

you look out your front windows down onto Michigan Avenue at exactly eleven o'clock you'll see something that should interest you."

That was the time when I figured we should be approaching the Lexington.

"What's up?" he asked, curiosity in his tone.

"Just take a look and you'll see," I answered curtly.

Then I slammed the receiver down and walked back into the garage, a pleased smile on my face. He'd look, I knew, and not knowing exactly what to expect, he'd have plenty of his goons on hand with him.

"Let's roll 'em!" I yelled, jumping into the lead car driven by Lahart.

The truck motors thundered into life, backfiring and coughing smoke, and we led the way out into the morning sunshine.

It was quite a parade.

We had little trouble staying together because traffic was light. Also, our drivers had orders to stay practically bumper to bumper. And we came to the Lexington at exactly eleven o'clock, I noted with pleasure as our car drew even with the hotel marquee and Marty wheeled it in against the curb. Chapman and Gardner took over to lead the trucks past in a thundering procession.

We had attracted an even better "house" than I had dared to expect.

In front of the Lexington was a cluster of the pearl gray hats. Cold eyes surveyed Marty and me as we braked to a halt, but then they forgot us as the motorcade slowly rumbled past.

"Keep it down to about fifteen miles an hour," I had

directed Chapman, and he was following orders to the letter.

My eyes were riveted on the knot of mobsters standing open-mouthed in the hotel entrance. Gesturing wildly, they began to jabber among themselves and I knew that they were recognizing individual vehicles on which they had probably ridden convoy recently.

One of the mob, a tall, thin man with a pock-marked face, said something to a dapper man standing beside him and they started forward as if to head for a car parked just behind us. Quickly, very ostentatiously, I raised the sawed-off shotgun from my lap and, as if by accident, rapped the stubby barrel against the metal doorpost.

The two hoodlums' attention was attracted by the sharp noise of clashing metal. They looked out of curiosity, their eyes widened and they moved back to join the cluster in front of the doorway. Their agitated whispers focused all eyes on us momentarily, but soon the trucks claimed their attention again.

Friel and King were past us now and the last fifteen trucks were belching noisily along in front of the Lexington. Leaning out of the window, I looked up toward the top floors from where I knew Capone must be watching.

From each window, heads jutted. Arms pointed, puppet-like, making jerky motions. Al Capone and his amazed hoodlums had never seen such a show.

"I can't distinguish Capone but I don't imagine he's as happy as he should be to see all his trucks again," I said in an aside to the alert Lahart.

"Let 'em eat their hearts out," Marty grinned. "I just wish

205

one of these monkeys—or all of 'em, for that matter—would try to start something."

The tail gate of the last truck slid by and Seager nodded to us as the rear guard car, driven by Leeson, passed us at the end.

Marty and I continued to sit there while the rumble of our procession faded in the distance. The knot of hoodlums gathered in the doorway turned their stares in our direction and then, at a command from the tall, pock-marked man, began to disappear into the hotel. The last one, a nattily dressed little runt, spat in our direction, but when I shifted the sawed-off shotgun with a quick motion, he scuttled inside the door.

Lahart was laughing as I turned to him and said:

"Okay, son, take it away."

Our parade by this time had turned off Michigan Avenue and was heading back to the new garage. Knowing the route, we sped a few blocks farther on, coming out ahead of the lead car.

"Pull up at the corner," I told Marty, "and we'll watch 'em go by. This time I'd like to enjoy the whole parade without distraction, and we'll also be able to see whether anybody is tailing it."

Waving Chapman and Gardner on, we sat there and gloated. The cost to Capone of this rolling stock alone was a fantastic figure. After the entire procession had passed, we sat there quietly watchful but could detect no "tail."

"All right, Marty," I said finally. "Let's follow them home."

We trailed them to the new garage and watched with an anticlimactic feeling while the trucks pulled slowly inside and were parked in ordered ranks. Then I gathered my men and told them lunch was on me, adding my standard gag:

"All you can eat as long as you take the thirty-five-cent blue plate special."

The last time I had said that was the day "The Untouchables" were born. Since then the "Kid" had drifted into limbo, we had captured the killer with the dumdum bullets meant for me, Basile had been murdered and we had helped to nail his killer.

What we had done this day was certain to enrage the bloodiest mob in criminal history. But it would do much more than that, I thought. We had hurled the defiance of "The Untouchables" into their teeth; they surely knew by now that we were prepared for a fight to the finish.

I was in my office the next morning when the telephone rang. It was Bill Wallace, the stoolie we called "Willie the Whisper." His words were hurried and worried.

"If ya can meet me in the second floor men's room of the Boston Store at eleven-thirty this morning, I got some dope ya might be interested in."

His wanting to meet me in a department store washroom indicated that it wasn't very healthy these days to be seen talking to Eliot Ness.

"All right," I told him. "I'll be there."

Summoning Marty Lahart and Mike King, I told them about "Willie, the Whisper's" call.

"This could be a plant and I'd certainly hate to get chopped down in a men's room," I said. "So we'll show up about fifteen minutes early and case the washroom. Mike will hang around the counters outside and keep an eye on anybody who goes in. I'll go in first and Marty, you follow me in."

The washroom was empty when I opened the door and I was washing my hands when Lahart came in and disappeared into one of the stalls where he could watch the entrance through the crack in the door.

A few minutes before eleven-thirty, Willie came in furtively, and when he saw Marty's feet behind one of the doors his face paled and he pointed jerkily with his finger.

"It's okay," I told him. "He's with me."

Willie also ducked into a stall and half closed the door. His Adam's apple bobbed convulsively in his skinny neck as he peered cautiously out and began to talk urgently.

"Just thought ya'd like to know the 'Big Fella' almost threw a fit over that little truck caper of yours yesta'day. The way I get it from a guy who wuz there, he carried on like a ravin' maniac. He tears up and down, yellin' and screamin'—and he keeps yellin' 'I'll kill 'im! I'll kill 'im with my own bare hands!' He even takes a couple chairs and busts 'em all t'hell and gone over a table. The guy tells me. . ."

Willie broke off and disappeared behind the closing door of the stall as two men came into the washroom. They probably wouldn't be laughing like they were, I thought idly, if they knew that Lahart had them both covered with his .38 and that the little man who had followed them in was Mike King, ready to use his gun at the slightest wrong move.

I took a long time washing my hands until they left, followed out by Mike, savoring the picture of "Scarface Al" as he stormed through his headquarters breaking furniture like a man demented after viewing our parade of his trucks. I could see those hard brown eyes snapping yellow sparks, the thick lips peeled back in a snarl and the scar glaring whitely against his livid face.

208

When the two men left, Willie opened the door a trifle again.

"This guy tells me," Willie hurriedly picked right up where he had left off, "that they had a helluva time calming him down. They wuz all there: Frankie Rio, Ralph, Mops Volpe, Bomber Belcastro, Frank Nitti, Three-fingered Jack White and a flock of others. They jus' sat there like dummies 'til the 'Big Fella' wears hisself out. Then he starts all over again when Ralph tells him that they got enough trouble without knocking off you guys.

"Finally, they chase everybody else out of the joint and the last thing this guy hears is the 'Big Fella' saying 'I want that Ness and I want 'im dead, even if it's on the front steps of City Hall.'

"And that's about it," Willie gulped noisily.

Capone had really been upset, I thought with a chilled feeling as I gave Willie some money and left. In the years since his roughneck days, Capone had acquired a suave urbanity, leaving the killing to his hired hands. But after seeing our parade, he had reverted to the "Scarface Al" of old; the man who could fiendishly use a baseball bat to brain those he hated.

How much, I wondered, had his "board of directors" succeeded in calming him down? For the first and only time in my life, I hoped that a group of gangsters had succeeded.

Chapter 20

Because of the increasing violence, the United States District Attorney's office ordered a raid on the haunts of every known gangster in the Chicago Heights area.

The raid was planned for a Sunday morning, and we from the district attorney's office were supported by one hundred hand-picked Chicago detectives.

Our first move was to sweep down on and take over completely the red-brick-fronted Chicago Heights police station. If this had not been done, we were sure, hoodlums throughout the area would have been given the alarm from the police station itself.

We descended on the section like a plague of locusts, taking many prisoners, an arsenal of guns of every description, thousands of rounds of ammunition, baskets filled with knives and even a number of machine guns.

My special job on this raid was to capture Joe Martino, head of the local chapter of the Unione Siciliano and my old "friend" from the meeting with Johnny Giannini in Pete Scalonas' saloon.

Lahart and I headed straight for Martino's home, which was over the poolroom in which the "Clown" had seen the late and unlamented Tony Napoli receive the "kiss of death" benediction before he set out to murder Basile. Inside my coat pocket was a warrant for Martino's arrest on a liquor conspiracy charge.

As we approached the frame building, I told Marty:

"You go up the back stairs and I'll take the front. We shouldn't have any trouble, because I don't think Martino is the type to start spraying with a gun, but keep your eyes open."

"Will do," Marty replied, circling the building to take it from the rear.

The front entrance was adjacent to the poolroom entrance. There was a bell, but I tried the knob, and when it turned I pushed my way inside and stood facing a flight of carpeted stairs leading straight up to a door at the top.

Taking the steps two at a time, I reached the small landing and rapped on the door. I could hear children prattling inside and the shrill voice of a woman screeching at them. The door opened almost immediately and Martino stood there, face blanching as he recognized me.

"I want you, Joe," I said quietly. "I've got a federal warrant for your arrest on a liquor conspiracy charge. Don't make a fuss because there's no use having any trouble."

"No, no," he quavered. "No fuss, please. I was just going out so please come in while I get my hat."

Pushing in, I saw Marty coming in through a kitchen rich with the mouth-watering odor of Italian cooking, while several wide-eyed children crowded shyly behind the skirt of a portly woman with a frightened look on her face.

The room in which I stood surprised me with its gaudy opulence. Persian rugs graced the floors and there were rich drapes and tapestries on the walls. The furniture was solid mahogany. Marble busts and bronze figurines stood on pedestals and there were flowers in hand-painted bowls.

"All right, Momma," Martino said in the precise, accented way I remembered. "Everything is all right. Close the kitchen door."

The woman followed his directions obediently and Martino, his smooth face a pasty white, walked over to a closet. He didn't reach for the hat I could see on a shelf, but hunched over. I saw something drop into some overshoes, and Martino tried to kick it back into the corner.

Spinning him away from the closet, I directed Marty:

"Keep him covered."

Reaching down into the corner of the closet, my hand closed on something hard—a .45-caliber automatic.

Jamming it in my pocket, I whirled on him and said:

"You packing anything else, Joe?"

A quick search revealed nothing but his empty shoulder holster. Joe Martino didn't want to be taken in with a gun in his possession.

His face, meanwhile, had been getting even whiter. Suddenly he put his hands to his mouth and said in a strangled voice:

"I'm sick."

Without warning, he became ill, staining the rich, bright rug on which we were standing.

I couldn't help feeling a little sorry for him. He wasn't the violent type. I remembered that it was he who had attempted to call off the killer with the candy-striped shirt that night in Scalonas' saloon. And then, too, there were those wide-eyed kids on the other side of the kitchen door.

But Joe Martino was a gangster, a leader of the dreaded Maffia and, in all probability, one of those who had ordered the one-way ride for Basile. And I had a job to do, so I did it. Marty and I took him in.

Martino and the others we arrested stayed in jail all that day, and it wasn't until late the next afternoon that they finally were released on bail.

I thought of that portly, fearful woman and those innocent, wide-eyed kids when I heard the news.

Joe Martino went home to the Heights at four-thirty Monday afternoon. Two minutes later, as he prepared to enter his own front door, he was mowed down by a deadly burst of machine gun fire.

The Maffia is unrelenting and unforgiving. He had failed to take me out of circulation at the very beginning when, in the back room of a saloon on State Street, all he had to do was say "Yes! Yes!" instead of "No! No!"

Johnny Giannini, who had followed Martino's lead that night in Pete Scalonas' saloon and refrained from giving the death order, escaped our Sunday morning dragnet. I was certain that Giannini, a man with a long, cruel memory, had come out of hiding and in retribution ordered Martino to the grave.

Now, as we started to close in on them, we began to press for more positive evidence with which to support the conspiracy case.

Through our wire tap we had enough evidence against the

Montmartre Café to obtain a search warrant. What we needed were records, check stubs and other papers which would be admissible evidence in court.

Rounding up Lahart, Seager and Cloonan, a powerful trio on a raid where trouble well might be expected, I was besieged by Robsky to let him in, too.

"That back alley owes me a debt," he explained. " I lost ten years of my life going up that pole and putting in the wire tap."

So I included him, assigning him and Seager the job of crashing in from the alley while Marty, Barney and I rushed the front.

"Let's make it late in the day when Tony Marino is there," Marty begged. "That monkey made me sick during my great impersonation, always telling me what a big, tough guy he was. And I understand,—since the word got around that I wasn't just a bird in a gilded cage—that he's been bragging how he'd take care of me if he ever got the chance."

"Okay, if you want to do it the hard way, that's the way we'll do it," I grinned.

We set the time for five o'clock in the afternoon, primarily to accommodate Lahart.

Separating at the corner, I gave Seager and Robsky ten minutes in which to take their places in the alley where Paul and I had hidden the day we ran the wire tap. Then I moved up to the front door and was about to hammer for entrance when Lahart tugged at my arm.

"Let's not be too polite, chief."

Motioning me to step aside, he hoisted one big brogan and sent the door crashing open. We crowded into a heavily ornamented room in which there were half a dozen men and two women.

"Hold it just like that. This is a federal raid," Cloonan bellowed, waving his .45-caliber Smith and Wesson. "Everybody sit nice and quiet and nobody will get hurt."

"Well, almost nobody," Lahart's soft announcement came clearly through the room.

Then Marty tucked his revolver into his shoulder holster and walked over to a husky, black-haired dandy who I knew instinctively was Tony Marino.

"I understand you've been looking for me," Lahart grinned down at him. "Well, here I am and I'd like you to notice I put my gun away. Would you like to stand up and find out just how tough you are?"

Marino didn't move, dropping his eyes to the floor.

Reaching down, Marty hoisted him out of his chair and pushed a pugnacious jaw into Marino's face.

"Your breath stinks and so do you," Marty said, and when Marino still refused to look at him or make a move, Marty sighed deeply and open-handedly pushed Marino in the face. Marino collapsed back onto his chair like a deflated balloon.

Everyone in the room had been watching this little byplay, Barney's pistol and mine holding them motionless. Drawing his gun again, Marty turned and announced:

"They're all yellow unless you aren't looking."

By this time I had spotted the alcove behind the bar, and as I headed for it a bearish man with the build of a wrestler came through the partially closed drapes.

"Percy Haller," Marty told me.

"This is a federal raid," I told Haller.

His answer was quick and sneering.

"Where's your warrant?"

As I handed it to him he looked around quickly at his fellow hoodlums as if to prime them for action, then ripped it in half and dropped it on the floor.

Things could begin to happen in a moment, I knew. So there was only one way to deal with this arrogant brute who thought that his master Al Capone was bigger than the federal government.

Moving quickly, I switched my gun to my left hand and hit Haller on the chin, knocking him backward over one of the gleaming, black-topped tables. His body did a complete somersault, and he lay where he fell.

"And now," Cloonan roared, "do any of you other characters want any trouble?"

Apparently no one did, and as Marty began to collect their guns, Seager and Robsky came into the room prodding two of the pearl gray hats along in front of them. One of the hoodlums had the beginnings of a colossal black eye.

"I see you had to shake this one up a little," I said to Seager.

He shook his head and shot an admiring glance at Robsky.

"Nope," Sam protested. "We walked up to these goons and that one with the shiner started for his roscoe. Little Paul changed his mind with as fine a right hand as I've ever seen."

Robsky grinned thinly, and there was an icy edge to his voice:

"Now I'm even for that pole out back."

The thought raced through my mind that all of my men were getting trigger tempered. Their nerves were stretching so taut from the danger which hovered over them constantly that they were set to go off like time bombs. It figured, because I felt the same way. I knew that there had been more violence than absolutely necessary in the punch I landed on the still-unconscious Haller.

Lahart broke my train of thought as he brought Haller up sputtering by dumping an abandoned highball in his face. After herding the prisoners together, we began a search for records which could be used as incriminating evidence. We found plenty of it—stacked carefully in a wall cabinet in the alcove.

All of this material, naturally, had to be sorted over by Chapman in long hours of checking and cross-checking, filing and cross-filing. It was a backbreaking task, and he did a magnificent job.

It was now harder than ever to locate the breweries—or what was left of them.

We had closed more than thirty large plants, and seized forty-five trucks. We had smashed millions of dollars' worth of equipment and dumped an ocean of beer and alcohol down protesting drains.

With the major breweries practically out of business, as far as we could discover, we ran a wire tap in on Jake "Greasy Thumb" Guzik, the syndicate's harried treasurer, at the Wabash Hotel.

"Here's something that shows how bad business is getting," Friel told me one morning when he brought in a report on a telephone conversation Guzik had had with a parched customer.

The handwriting looked as beautiful to me as a Da Vinci. The words were music to my ears:

"Hello, Jake?"

"Yeah."

"This is Turk."

"Uh-huh."

"I ain't gettin' all the beer I can use."

"Nobody is. We just ain't got it."

"Well, I got to have more soon."

"Okay, okay. Keep your pants on. We're a little short but we're starting to ship some in from Indiana."

"Good. When do you expect it?"

"It should come in tomorrow night."

"Okay. Don't forget me."

"I won't. Don't worry."

"Okay. S'long."

That night we intercepted the load on its way into Chicago, capturing four huge trucks. "Greasy Thumb's" customers had something else to weep about, and so did the syndicate. Meanwhile, when they did manage to get a shipment past us, by keeping our tap on the Guzik headquarters at the Wabash we frequently were able to intercept deliveries to the speakeasies.

Chicago was drying up fast.

But so were our nerves. Ever since "Willie, the Whisper" had told me of Capone's violent rage after our "parade," I had been like a man waiting for the guillotine to fall.

So, too, had my men. I could perceive it in a hundred little ways. Lahart's laugh was not so spontaneous or hearty. Seager's eyes were never still; he never showed off his newest matchbox covers. It was noticeable in all of them, in the way they drummed with their fingers or felt for the revolvers in their shoulder holsters. The suspense was building up to such a head that I almost wished Capone would try something.

Chapter 21

Beer was practically nonexistent in Chicago when we struck our greatest blow at the syndicate by uncovering a gigantic alcohol plant worth a quarter of a million dollars and turning out twenty thousand gallons a day.

So tremendous was this operation that the output not only was shipped in carload lots of fifty-gallon drums but was pumped directly into railroad tank cars.

The tip came through an anonymous telephone call.

"I'd like to speak to Mr. Ness," a lady's voice said.

"This is he."

"Mr. Ness," she began, "I'm not going to give you my name, but I think maybe I have something that can help you. My husband told me that he heard from somebody that there is something funny going on in the plant of the Illinois Iron Company in the 1800 block on Diversey Avenue. They seem to think that maybe somebody is making beer or whisky or something there."

"What makes them think so?" I asked.

"Well, I don't know," she said. "That's why I'm telling you to find out. It's about time somebody made this a decent city for us sober, hard-working people, and I just think you ought to look into it. So see that you do."

With that, she slammed the phone down in my ear.

We had received a number of anonymous tips as the months went by, some good and some completely unfounded. But none of them was overlooked; in each case, I, myself, or one of my men, would make a discreet but thorough check before we decided whether or not to conduct a raid.

I told Lahart about the woman who had called and asked him to accompany me on a tour of inspection.

We drove out Diversey and finally came to the plant; a large sign proclaimed it to be the Illinois Malleable Iron Company. The huge six-story building looked exactly as advertised. I directed Marty to park in front of the building while I walked inside to take a close look.

A wide counter and, behind it, a number of women clerical workers indicated that this was a legitimate operation. When one of the women approached, I smiled innocently and asked:

"Could you tell me where the Lahart Lamp Factory is located?"

There being no such company in Chicago, as far as I knew, I was certain that the young lady couldn't tell me. But my intention was to lure her into conversation.

"No," she puzzled thoughtfully, "I don't believe I ever heard of it. Do you know the address?"

I told her I thought it was in the 1800 block on Diversey.

"No," she said positively, "It isn't around here or I would know about it."

"Are you sure?" I asked. "Have you worked here long?"

"I certainly am sure," she bridled. "I've been here three years and I know this whole neighborhood."

"I'm sorry, I didn't mean to offend you," I smiled. "Why, I didn't even know they employed pretty girls in an iron plant."

She simpered and, looking around, I observed in pseudo amazement:

"This certainly is a big place. Do they make iron all the way up to the top of the building? And if so, how do they get it down?"

"Oh, no," she replied. "Our company just uses the first four floors. There's another firm on the two top floors and they make paint—or something. But they've only been up there a few months."

"Well," I told her, "thanks a lot for your help. I guess I'd better get looking for that lamp company."

As I left the building, I saw an adjoining door. There was no name lettered on it and I found that it was locked.

"There's something peculiar there," I observed, back in the car. "If it is a legitimate paint company, that might explain our anonymous tipster's olfactory suspicion that they were making alcohol. Then, too, it seems improbable that such an obviously legitimate firm as Illinois Iron would permit a still to be operated on its premises. And, to boot, how would whoever is running the still get the stuff down?"

But at the back of my mind were the questions of why a legitimate paint company did not have its name lettered on the downstairs door, and why that door should be locked during business hours.

Finally I turned to Lahart and said:

"Marty, I noticed an iron fire escape in the side court that goes all the way up to the top of that building. Tonight we're going back there and take a close look at that paint company."

"Oh, well," Marty yawned, "I was getting tired of that pipe and carpet slippers routine, anyhow."

Impatiently, I waited for evening to come. When something like this took a grip on me, I felt just as I did when, as a boy, I waited for the opening performance of the circus after it came to town.

During "bootleg hours," long after dark, Marty and I drove out Diversey again and parked about two blocks from the plant. We had planned to approach it from the rear, but stumbling down a spur track of the North Western Railroad tracks, we saw a bright light beaming in the rear of the building and were forced to retreat. Our only course was to approach it from the front, and as we did we saw lights in the windows on the upper two floors.

"I'm going up that fire escape," I told Marty. "If they're honest, we shouldn't get into any trouble. If they're not, trouble's what we're looking for, anyhow."

Marty boosted me up until I could catch the counterbalance which dropped the ladder. As I swung it down, the rusty iron made a tremendous screech. Breathlessly we waited, fearful that the noise might have been heard, but when nobody appeared I whispered to Marty:

"Here we go!"

Up we climbed, taking great care to move quietly; the rusted railings tore at our clothes and stained our hands. I swore softly as a jagged piece punctured the palm of my hand, but forgot the pain as my eyes drew level with the fifth-floor window sill and I looked into the lighted room within.

What I had smelled while climbing those last few yards had not been paint. And what I was looking at was not paint-manufacturing apparatus.

It was a giant alcohol still whose columns rose forty feet into the air and stretched through a hole cut into the ceiling or floor, depending on how you looked at it, between the fifth and sixth floors.

"Wow!" Marty breathed softly into my ear, "Would you take a look at that!"

It was by far the largest still either of us had ever seen, and we classed ourselves as experts in that department.

This was a mammoth operation, I realized as I watched six men working busily at various tasks in a floor space that stretched one hundred and twenty-five feet in both length and width. Two men operated an electrical lift, which was similar to that used in grain elevators. From the ground they hoisted large sacks of what I suspected to be corn sugar, used in the making of mash, and on the return trip to the railroad siding below they lowered an endless chain of loaded fifty-gallon drums.

I had seen enough. Now I wanted to get away before we were discovered.

As we turned to make our way down the fire escape, Marty froze and clamped a hand on my arm.

"Hold it!" he whispered tensely. "Look!"

Coming around the rear corner far below us, apparently on routine patrol, were two of the pearl gray hats. They moved out of the light cast from the loading platform and disappeared into the darkness underneath. I wondered belatedly whether we had drawn up the fire escape ladder, and then remembered that we had. Rigidly we huddled back tight against the side of the building and then, a few minutes later, apparently satisfied that all was well, the two figures reappeared in the cone of light and moved out of sight in the rear.

"Let's get out of here," I breathed softly.

Cautiously we climbed downward. Then, fearful that another squeak from that ladder might bring the guards, we hung by our hands, dropping into the side courtyard.

"Phew, that was close," Marty said when we had cleared the building. "It would have been a shame if they had seen us."

The next day we laid our plans carefully, bringing the whole group in on the raid. Each man drew an exact assignment, because we had long since learned to leave nothing to chance. This time, of course, with the plant high up on the fifth and sixth floors, we could not use our favored method of smashing through the doors in our truck.

We arranged it so that Marty and I would go up the fire escape and be in position to enter through the windows at the appointed time. I assumed that there would be both a freight elevator and stairs in the back, so Seager, Leeson, Robsky, King and Cloonan were detailed to approach from the rear while Gardner, Chapman and Friel attacked from the front.

"Sam," I told Seager, "you and Leeson take the freight elevator while Robsky and King move up the stairs. That leaves Barney to cover the back from the landing platform just in case there is a way out through the iron works."

They nodded and I turned to Chapman.

"Lyle," I said, "will crash the front door and take Friel up the stairs with him. Gardner will remain down front and cover there in case someone tries to get out through the iron works. Meanwhile, Marty and I will crack in from the windows on the fifth and sixth floors."

It was close to midnight—and I was thankful that there was no moon—when we approached the huge building and parked several blocks away. Then we split up, Seager leading his squad down a side street to the railroad spur and noiselessly beginning his infiltration so that at the designated time we could attack simultaneously.

This time Marty and I were equipped with a small ladder so that we would not have to use the squeaking fire escape ladder. Together with Gardner, Chapman and Friel, we approached the front cautiously. Gardner and Chapman melted into the shadows near by, safe from the eyes of any chance patrol, and after a hasty look to make certain that nobody was in the side court we whisked in, planted the ladder, and Marty and I began our cautious climb. As we gained the fire escape, Friel removed the ladder and disappeared with it into the street.

Once again Marty and I were climbing up those rusty stairs, encumbered this time with our sawed-off shotguns. It was two minutes to midnight when we reached the fifth-floor landing. Motioning Marty up to the sixth floor with a jerk of my thumb, I peered inside to make certain that he wasn't seen as he climbed quickly through the light glare from the window and reached the slatted iron perch above my head.

I could see my watch easily in the glare from the window, and as the hands closed together I stood up, whistled shrilly and smashed the window with a slashing blow of my shotgun. Up above I could hear Marty doing the same as I lowered my head, held my arms in front of my face and leaped through in a shower of glass to the floor inside.

Four men stood slack jawed and stunned as I covered them with the sawed-off shotgun and called:

"This is a federal raid. Don't make a move!"

They raised their hands and stood quietly as I advanced on them. Within seconds, Marty came down a flight of inside stairs, pushing a fifth man along with the barrel of his shotgun.

"That's all that's up on the sixth floor," he said.

Within a few minutes, Robsky and King came charging in, panting from their headlong dash up the stairs. Chapman and Friel were gasping, too, as they joined us from the front. There was a grinding noise from the freight elevator as it jolted to a stop.

"It's a lot easier this way," Seager said, flashing one of his rare smiles as he noticed the heaving chests of those who had to make it hurriedly on foot. Leeson leaned against the back of the cage easily and nodded his agreement, his sawed-off shotgun trained on the white-faced elevator operator.

Now, with plenty of time to take a full inventory, I saw that this, without doubt, was the most staggering setup I had ever seen. The giant still was geared to turn out the almost unbelievable total of twenty-thousand gallons a day. Certainly this amount couldn't be moved in fifty-gallon drums.

Lahart solved that puzzle when he called me to the back end of the vast room.

"Look here," he whistled, "pipes which must lead right to those tank cars on the siding."

That's exactly what they were, and further investigation disclosed that there also was an entire carload of empty fifty-gallon drums waiting below to be unloaded. A series of tremendous vats on the upper floor contained the amazing total of one hundred and twenty thousand gallons of mash.

There was another innovation, we discovered as we made an inventory. Up until this time, corn sugar had been the basic product used to make alcohol mash. But the mob on this operation had discovered a new and more efficient material, the mash for this giant still being made from hydrol, a mixture of grain and sugar.

Subsequent investigation disclosed that the still had been in operation almost six months without the workers in the iron company below ever becoming suspicious. I often wondered whether the mysterious female tipster was one of the women working downstairs. However, regardless of who she was, she had done us a tremendous favor. Estimating that approximately four hundred and eighty thousand gallons of alcohol had been shipped from the plant, with each gallon bringing the mob two dollars profit, we came to the conclusion that they had netted close to one million dollars in that brief period of operation.

This was another backbreaking blow to the mob's financial situation. They would sorely miss the lucrative income they had been receiving from the cooker in the sky.

Two days later, when I reached my car just after leaving the office, the snap flew open on my brief case, and in exasperation I steadied it on the fenders as I refastened the snap. As I did, I noticed that the hood of the car was slightly open. A quick glance showed me that both hooks were unfastened.

If only one hook had been unfastened, I might not have paid any particular attention. But an alarm bell began to ring somewhere in the back of my head, and very cautiously I raised the hood.

Attached to the wiring system just under the thin panel separating the driver's seat from the motor was a dynamite bomb. I carefully lowered the hood and called the police.

"If you had just touched that starter," said the police department explosives expert as he removed it gingerly from the car, "you'd have been blown to kingdom come."

So I'd been lucky again. "But how long can such luck last?" I asked myself as I wiped a clammy forehead with my handkerchief. I sat there in the car a long time after the police left. The reaction had set in and I had to press my legs together to keep them from trembling. That had been close, too close, and at that moment it was small solace to know that we had reduced the mob to such desperate measures.

Chapter 22

Shortly after the raid which netted the giant still high above the iron company, we learned that we definitely had forced the mob's hand.

We had run a tap on "Greasy Thumb" Guzik's telephone at the Wabash earlier and had recorded an interesting bit of conversation between the mob's treasurer and a caller named Hymie.

We ascertained that he was Hymie Levine, who ran a secondhand automobile parts shop. Behind this legitimate façade, Levine was actually one of the mob's pay-off men. It was he who dealt with those among the police who were receiving protection pay-offs for closing their eyes to the mob's activities.

Without exciting suspicion, the police could filter into Levine's shop and he would check with Guzik by telephone to find out how much they were to receive. The typical conversation went like this:

"Jake, this is Hymie. Lieutenant Sands is here. How much does he get?"

There would be a brief pause, apparently while Guzik thumbed through his police protection list, and then his voice would reply:

"He's okay. His bite is fifty bucks."

As the weeks went by, we had compiled a list of several policemen who were on the mob's pay roll. The pay-offs, which fluctuated, ranged from five dollars a week for an ordinary patrolman to as high as a thousand dollars for a four-man detective squad.

This information was turned over to my friend Captain Schoemaker for subsequent house-cleaning action, and Chapman also included a detailed report in our extensive conspiracy file.

So it came as extremely welcome news to me when, after closing the giant alcohol still, Robsky came in one morning and slid a sheet of paper with penciled notes on it in front of me.

"Here's the latest from the Wabash wire tap," he chuckled. "I was certain that this one you would want to see!"

Thanking him, my eyes skimmed down the page. The words that recounted a recent phone conversation between Guzik and Levine were a citation to our efforts.

The conversation went:

"Jake? This is Hymie."

"Yeah, Hymie?"

"Lieutenant Sands is in again. What's he get?"

"Nothin'."

"Whatta ya mean, nothin'?"

231

"Listen, Hymie, you'll have to tell the boys they'll have to take a pass this month."

"They ain't gonna like it!"

"Too bad, but we just ain't makin' any dough. And if we ain't got it, we can't pay it."

"Well, if that's the way it's gotta be, that's the way it's gotta be."

"You're damned right. Just tell 'em that."

"Okay. S'long."

The job for which we had been selected was getting done. We had been told to close up the breweries and shut off their revenue: this was concrete proof that we were accomplishing our mission.

"We've got them on the run," I told Robsky. "Now let's hammer the final nails in their coffin."

We worked with renewed vigor. Nothing was too small for our attention. We were running them out of dollars, and now I even wanted their nickels and dimes.

Day after day we raided liquor caches and speak-easies. We were receiving a great deal of newspaper publicity and the anonymous telephone tips kept pouring in. Typical of these calls was one in which the informant, a man who refused to identify himself, simply said:

"Why don't you guys take a look at a garage at 2640 South Wells Street?"

Before I could say a word, the caller hung up.

That night we closed in on the garage, smashed down the doors and found a twenty-five-thousand-dollar-supply of imported whisky and other liquors. The garage obviously was used as a warehouse to supply the syndicate's liquor cutting plants. It housed three hundred and eighty cases of bonded whisky, four hundred and sixty five gallon jugs of bourbon, several dozen cases of champagne and several cases of assorted cordials and liquors.

Several days later, another anonymous tipster alerted us to a garage at 3419 North Clark Street.

He rang off before I could even thank him.

We swooped down on the garage and used a crowbar to force the wide double doors. As the hasp gave I pushed inside, with Lahart and Leeson behind me, and stopped short in dismay. The garage, large enough for two cars, was completely empty. The walls were bare and the ceiling was merely a skeleton framework of supporting beams. Nothing could be hidden up there.

Disgustedly I stood there and shoved my hands into my pockets. My fingers began toying with a fifty-cent piece in one pocket, and as I gave Lahart and Leeson a frustrated shrug of the shoulders, I flipped it into the air, catching the spinning coin as it descended.

"Looks like a real blank," Marty said.

His voice distracted my attention, and I missed the coin. Falling to the floor with a sharp, ringing sound, it cartwheeled straight across the concrete and disappeared into an iron grating set flush with the floor in the gloomy far corner of the garage.

Through the openings in the grill, I could see my coin lying on what looked like the top of a wooden case.

"Give me a hand with this grating," I told Lahart and Leeson.

They came over and we lifted out the ironwork, fitted snugly into a large opening which ordinarily we would have assumed to be a drainage outlet, and there below us, packed neatly under the concealing grill, we found a twelve-foot chamber. And in that chamber were one hundred cases of the finest imported liquors, later valued at fifteen thousand dollars.

If it hadn't been for that lucky roll of that spinning coin we probably would have walked out of the garage without locating the hidden cache.

Soon afterwards, we had another indication of the mob's desperate straits: they began using regular passenger cars to deliver a mere three or four barrels of beer where once they had boldly driven huge vans loaded with barrels through the streets of Chicago.

This development was discovered during a watch on Manley's Night Club at 2300 South State Street. We stood in an alleyway and observed two men roll two barrels of beer out of a Ford coach from which all the seats except the driver's had been removed. Marty and I walked right in the back door, just behind the men rolling the barrels, and took them into custody. Then we forced them to roll the barrels out into the alley and we stove in the sides with an ax.

It was quite obvious now, when the syndicate was down to delivering a mere two barrels of imported beer in ordinary passenger cars, that the city was extremely arid. So we turned our attention to drying up the area surrounding the city.

I told Mike King: "Cover the railroad shipping offices and track down any shipments of corn sugar. Take Leeson with you and have him follow any substantial deliveries of corn sugar sacks."

While they instituted this new investigative procedure, the rest of us roamed the city with alert eyes, watching for the unusual. One afternoon, as Lahart and I were riding along

Calumet Avenue, we halted at an intersection beside a dilapidated ice truck bearing a full load. The driver looked over at us, and when he saw me he started and looked swiftly away. His actions aroused in me a vague suspicion.

"Speed ahead," I told Marty. "Circle the block and come up behind this ice truck again. I think this bird is up to something."

Lahart slammed the car into gear and we shot ahead, turning at the next corner and making a complete run around the block. Then we tailed the truck, careful to stay far enough back so that we would not be noticed. After a few blocks, the truck turned left, pulled into an alley and drew to a halt behind 2636 Calumet Avenue. We continued on past the alley entrance and parked a short distance away, walking back just as the truck lurched into motion again and pulled through the doors of a large double garage.

Swiftly we walked toward the garage. As we approached it, a man busily closing the doors spotted us while we still were about twenty-five yards away. Leaving the doors ajar, he ducked back quickly inside the garage and we began to race toward the entrance. Bursting in through the doors, we saw three men running through a small door at the far end of the garage. Marty and I set out in pursuit. By the time we hurled ourselves through the doorway they had reached the alley and were racing toward the street where we had parked our car. We pounded after them, but two of them disappeared into another alleyway across the street and the third one, a short, stout man, fled up the street in the opposite direction from the car.

"I'll get this one," I panted. "You get back to that garage

and make sure they don't circle around and clean out anything that might be there."

Lahart spun about and headed back toward the garage while I darted in pursuit of the fat man, who now headed into Calumet Avenue, his short legs churning. Racing to the corner, I saw a police patrol car idling along slowly. Waving it toward me, I leaped on the running board and shouted to the officer who was driving:

"Overtake that man! He's a federal fugitive!"

The patrol car leaped forward. Looking back over his shoulder, the man ran toward an alleyway. We were almost abreast of him as he scurried into the narrow passage, and I leaped from the running board and sprinted in after him. He was racing ahead of me, knocking garbage cans over into my path, so I drew my .38 and fired two quick shots over his head. Panic stricken, he skidded to a halt and backed up against a high board fence, hands in the air. His chest was heaving and I thought from the way he was wheezing and the bloodless look on his face that if he had run any farther he might have collapsed with a heart attack.

Turning him over to the policeman who had followed me into the alley, I hurriedly made my way back to the garage. Marty stood in front of the ice trucks.

"Well, Paavo Nurmi," Marty laughed, mentioning the name of the great Finnish runner, "while you've been galloping hither and yon I have discovered a nice little kettle of suds."

Pulling back the tarpaulin from a three-ton truck in the garage, Marty bared a load of iced-down half barrels of beer all ready for delivery to the week-end trade. Stowed in a corner of the garage under another greasy tarpaulin were a number of large barrels of beer.

It wasn't long after this that the work of King and Leeson in watching the railroad shipments of corn sugar began to show signs of success. Mike spotted one large load, and he and Leeson tailed the truck carrying the sacks of corn sugar to a farm at near-by Dundee, Illinois. When the truck turned into a dusty lane and headed for a huge barn, our men continued past and then circled back. Crawling through the fields, they set up a watch on the barn, and after a while saw the emptied truck leave.

That night we raided the barn and thought at first that we had made a mistake because, upon entering, all we saw were long rows of stalls in which more than forty cows were contentedly chewing their cuds. But above the odor of the usual barn smells we detected the aroma made only by a still.

It was up in the loft. There we found a 750-gallon still, another 250-gallon still, 15 tanks of mash, 6,500 pounds of sugar and 820 gallons of finished alcohol. Six men on the premises were taken into custody.

"What are we going to do about the cows?" demanded the farmer who owned the animals and also operated the stills. "If we can't get bail by morning, somebody's gonna have to milk these critters."

"Don't look at me," I told him. "I never milked a cow in my life and I wouldn't know which spigot to turn."

"Well, somebody's gonna have to milk 'em," he insisted.

That was the one and only time I was glad to see our prisoners arrange a speedy bail bond. It saved us considerable embarrassment because, of our whole crew, only Leeson had ever milked a cow.

237

The Untouchables

After that raid, Leeson and King began to carry binoculars in their car to facilitate their spying from a distance on any isolated farmhouses that might come under suspicion. And it wasn't long before they needed them.

King spotted another big shipment of corn sugar which he and Joe tailed to a ramshackle farm near Blue Island, Illinois. It took them several trips before they followed it all the way home because the driver apparently was suspicious and did a great deal of circling before he finally turned off at a dirt road and jounced half a mile to a farm. The truck pulled up to a barn behind the house and the sacks were carried inside.

King and Leeson drove along until they came to another dirt road some distance away and followed it to a high spot from which they could survey the entire area. There they set up an observation post in a clump of trees, Mike climbing to the top of an oak tree and observing the barn through the binoculars. They kept their vigil for several days before the truck drove into the yard again and three men started unloading a large supply of gleaming five-gallon cans.

That night we arranged the raid. Turning off our headlights as we drove onto the bumpy dirt road, we inched our way forward until we were within several hundred feet of the farmhouse. Leaving the cars there, we surrounded both the farmhouse and the barn and then closed in.

There were no animals in this barn, I noticed with some relief. Instead, there were two six-hundred-gallon stills, both of them "cooking," twenty tanks of mash, a thousand pounds of corn sugar and more than a thousand gallons of finished alcohol. Only one man was there, and he surrendered without a struggle.

238

Meanwhile, Lahart and several of the others had invaded the farmhouse by both the front and back doors.

"Only one guy in there," Marty reported. "But there are beds where at least half a dozen guys have been sleeping. Some of them must have gone to town."

"Well, let's wait awhile and maybe they'll come back," I said, directing Leeson, King and Robsky to go get our cars and drive them behind the barn. Then, if any cars approached, they wouldn't be seen.

We had been in the farmhouse only a short time, while Chapman made an inventory in the barn, when Friel, who had been posted as a lookout to watch the dirt road leading up to the house, slipped in and said:

"A car just turned in off the main road and is heading toward the house."

Beckoning Friel to follow me, I slipped out the back door and we hurried around the house and down the dark lane about twenty yards. There we took up positions on either side of the road in two clumps of shrubbery which I had noted earlier.

The car slowed as it neared the house and pulled up beside the front porch. Two men alighted without any attempt at silence. One of them was speaking in a voice which carried clearly through the night.

"Go in the house and get Patsy, if he's in there," he said. "I want to tell him where to deliver the next load of alky."

The words were no sooner spoken than Friel and I slid up behind them. Then, covering them with our guns, called out:

"Stick 'em up. We're government officers and this is a federal raid."

As I said this, Lahart stepped out of the front door and caught the two men in the beam of a large flashlight.

What we had apprehended, complete wtih uniforms, was a pair of deputy sheriffs.

"Don't shoot," one of them trembled. "What you want is hanging right here on my belt."

I moved forward and relieved them of their revolvers. The taller one, apparently the ringleader, was wearing one of the fanciest guns I had ever seen. It was an ivory-handled, nickel-plated .38 with a pair of carved fox heads on the gleaming white butt. They confessed freely that the still was their operation, and the two men we had taken prisoner earlier attested to this.

The word spread throughout the ranks of the underworld that "The Untouchables" now were raiding far and wide. Even the railroad shipments of corn sugar petered out and the Chicago area, to all intents and purposes, had become as dry as the proverbial bone.

Evidence of this developed when Captain Schoemaker, now the Chief of Detectives, picked up Bert Delaney. The one-time Capone brewmaster, with whom we had frequently tangled, complained bitterly that he was "working for a living as a trucker."

"Shoes" chuckled when he repeated Delaney's remark.

"Why pick me up?" Delaney asked Schoemaker aggrievedly. "One time I was in the bucks. Now the racket is done. Eliot Ness of the feds has put Capone out of the beer and alky business and everybody else has just about folded up, too. There's no more money in anything crooked."

Those were some of the nicest words I had ever heard, and not just because it looked as if our job was about completed.

They were comforting words because they gave me a hope-
ful feeling that the period of our greatest personal danger was
past.

Capone was capable, of course, of ordering our execution
for sheer revenge. But with court actions getting under way
against him, I reasoned he would not want to make things
worse for himself by having any federal men murdered. At
least, telling myself this made it easier to breathe normally
after weeks of practically holding my breath. And from time
to time I found myself praying that I had it reasoned correctly.

Chapter 23

Now the legal gears finally began to mesh, and like the mills of the gods they ground exceedingly thin. With the records we had seized in our raids providing much of the evidence, Ralph Capone and Jake "Greasy Thumb" Guzik were snared on income tax charges which netted them respective three- and five-year prison sentences.

Then I was called before the grand jury as it met for a solid week. It was a sensation when, on June 12, 1931, indictments were handed down against Al Capone and sixty-eight others, charging them with five thousand violations of the prohibition laws on the heels of an income tax evasion indictment against Capone himself.

Capone already had been freed in $50,000 bail on the income tax indictment charging him with failure to pay $215,000 in taxes on an income of $1,050,000 in the years from 1924 through 1929. This bail was permitted to stand on both charges.

"It looks like we're coming to the end of the road," I told Betty that night as I picked her up for an evening's celebration. "If we get Capone, the whole thing will be broken."

Her eyes were misty and tender.

"I know, dear, and I'll be so glad when it is over," she said softly. "I've been worried for you for too long a time now. But I'm pretty proud of you, too."

She opened her handbag and produced a newspaper clipping.

"A girl friend of mine in Boston sent me this clipping from the Boston *Traveler,*" she smiled brightly.

The clipping was an editorial headed THE BIG SHOT WHIMPERS:

SCARFACE AL CAPONE IS IN A CORNER

The head of a ring that has cleaned up nearly a billion dollars in the past ten years whines as he sees the net closing about him. The government has charges against him which, if proved, make Capone liable to $90,000 in fines and thirty-four years in prison.

Capone faces charges of wholesale violation of the liquor laws and evasion of income tax. The government has been building up its case for years by the hardest kind of work and in the face of grave danger to its agents.

One young federal agent getting $2,800 a year played a prominent part in getting evidence on Capone. He was threatened, attacked, offered bribes and consistently stalked, yet on he worked, content with his $2,800 a year and his conscience. His name is no secret. Gangsters know it. He is Eliot Ness, graduate of the University of Chicago.

Capone has cause to whimper. His brother Ralph is doing a three-year stretch. His cousin Frank Nitti is in for 18 months. Jake Guzik, Capone's "business manager," has been given a five-year sentence. Others of the Capone gang face prison terms.

The bigshot turns out to be just a greaseball. He tried his guns against the power of the people. He got away with it for a while but his doom was sealed the minute he started it.

Returning the clipping to Betty with what must have been a slightly fatuous grin, I chuckled:

"Big man, huh?"

"Don't be embarrassed," she said seriously. "You deserve the praise and besides, it gives me hope that soon now you'll be able to return to a normal life and maybe I'll see a lot more of you."

"That's a promise," I told her. "And it shouldn't be too long now, either, the way things are going."

I didn't realize that it would be another eleven months until we saw the last of Al Capone.

Five of those months, interspersed with frequent court appearances, were spent tracking down George Howlett, one of the sixty-eight others named with Capone in the prohibition law violations.

Howlett, who also was wanted by the government on charges of evading $52,850 in income taxes, was known as Capone's "society lieutenant." He had lived a Jekyll and

Hyde existence by posing as the vice-president of a large Chicago printing firm while actually being one of the upper echelon of the Capone mob.

Nabbing him was one of our last major arrests.

Chapter 24

"Scarface Al" Capone, meanwhile, was fighting a last ditch battle with the law.

When I had walked from the grand jury room, I knew by the angry, dedicated looks on the jurors' faces that indictments would be returned. Four days after they were handed down, on June 12, 1931, the gangster overlord walked into court and pleaded guilty to charges of violating the liquor laws as well as income tax evasion.

A disdainful sneer still dominated the pale, flabby face with the flaming scar on the cheek. Al Capone thought he was going to be able to make a "deal" with the government.

His attorneys had offered a settlement of four million dollars on the income tax charges and were trying to "bargain" for a token jail term which, Capone boasted openly, would not exceed two and a half years.

I seethed inwardly at what could easily become a shallow victory for the law and could put Capone back in circulation very soon. Capone was treating the whole business lightly, like a man certain of reprieve. He attended the races, holding court in a front box. He bought expensive new suits, ordering the tailors to make the right pocket "extra large and double lined." And he was still surrounded by his usual entourage of well-heeled gunmen.

But I felt like standing up and cheering in the solemn quiet of the courtroom when, on July 30, 1931, Federal Judge James H. Wilkerson sharply told Capone and his startled lawyers that he refused to respect any "bargains."

I was standing in the corridor when Capone, resplendent in a dark green suit, matching accessories and brown-and-white sport shoes, appeared at the federal building to hear his expectedly light sentence.

"I'm a little nervous," Capone told newspapermen. "After all, I'm only human."

That, I thought as he pushed his way into the courtroom, was merely one man's opinion.

Capone's genial smile faded and he began to chew gum furiously when, as the proceedings opened, Judge Wilkerson boomed:

"I will hear the evidence in this case. And the defendant," he barked, looking straight at Capone, "must understand that he cannot have an agreement in this court."

The jurist listened attentively as United States District Attorney George E. Q. Johnson explained that the leniency recommendation which had been broadcast sneeringly by Capone had been arrived at with the approval of the attorney general, the head of the intelligence unit of the Internal Revenue Department and an assistant secretary of the Treasury.

Capone's jaws worked madly on his chewing gum, eyes

shuttling hastily from the judge back to his attorneys as the significance of what was transpiring came home to him.

"A plea of guilty is a full admission of guilt," the judge's voice interrupted. "The power of compromise is not vested in this court, but is conferred by Congress on other governmental offices. The court may require the production of evidence. If the defendant asks leniency by throwing himself on the mercy of the court he must be prepared to answer all proper questions put to him by the court. While the court may determine the degree of guilt, it must assume, on the defendant's plea, that the defendant committed the offenses as stated in the indictment."

Capone, I noted, made an effort to get back the rhythm of his gum chewing but gave it up. His jaws clamped tight and a little muscle jumped in his cheek as he stared at the judge. Wilkerson was speaking slowly and distinctly now, without heat, but with obvious emphasis aimed directly at Capone.

"If the defendant expects leniency from this court he must take the witness stand and testify on what grounds he expects leniency!"

Michael Ahern, Capone's counsel, stepped to the bench and his voice rose in protest:

"The defendant and his counsel never considered that this would be an unqualified plea. Prior to the entry of the plea and prior to the return of the last indictment, I conferred with the district attorney. The district attorney said if a plea of guilty was entered he would made a recommendation with respect to the duration of the punishment."

Judge Wilkerson held up his hand.

"I understand that the district attorney intends to do that."

Ahern continued swiftly.

"We thought that the recommendation would be approved by the court. We believed that the department would have the power to compromise both the criminal and civil liability, that it constituted an inducement for the defendant to enter the plea we made. I am frank to say that we would not have entered those pleas unless we thought the court would accept them as made."

Judge Wilkerson's voice left no room for debate.

"The defendant must understand that the punishment has not been decided before the close of the hearing. I must have it understood that there can be no bargaining in the federal court."

Watching Capone's face, while his attorney moved to withdraw the guilty plea, I knew that this scar-faced man who for years had scorned the law was realizing at last the fact that ultimately he couldn't "beat the rap."

Nor did he. Three months later he was convicted as charged, and on October 24, 1931, Judge Wilkerson sentenced him to eleven years in prison with a fine of fifty-thousand dollars.

More than six months went by as his attorneys fought through an appeal, but it was denied and on May 3, 1932, we gathered our forces to make certain that nothing would prevent the law from putting "Scarface Al" Capone on the Dixie Flyer for his trip to the Atlanta Penitentiary.

A pair of United States marshals were to take him to Atlanta, but we were to provide the protection until they had the prisoner safely aboard the train. I was determined to see there would be no "rescue" or that no assassin's bullet would cheat the law. We arranged a five-car caravan to escort "Snorkey" from the Cook County jail to the old Dearborn Station.

Lahart, Seager and I were to ride in the first car. Behind it was to be the car with Capone, followed by Robsky, Cloonan and King in another, followed by two automobiles carrying Chicago policemen. All of us were heavily armed: my crew was ready with sawed-off shotguns, revolvers and automatics loose in shoulder holsters.

By nine-thirty that night there was a tense air of expectancy, although the Dixie Flyer didn't depart until eleven-thirty. As Capone was led into the warden's office, the shouts of other prisoners echoed down the jail corridors.

"You got a bum break, Al!"

"Keep your chin up, Al—it ain't so tough!"

"You'll own the joint before you're there very long, Al!"

The United States marshals arrived at nine-thirty. Everything was prepared for our dash to the train, and Marshal Henry Laubenheimer handed the jail clerk the warrant which instructed the sheriff to "deliver the bodies of one Alphonse Capone and one Vito Morici."

Then they brought in Morici, who was being sent to Florida to be tried in the federal courts there for transporting a stolen car. Morici was a swarthy young man in a baggy gray suit and battered shoes. As he started to don a ragged gray topcoat, Capone barked:

"Keep that over your arm so nobody sees the handcuffs."

The two were manacled together, and I led the way into the jail's inner courtyard where a horde of photographers went into action, their flashbulbs exploding with blinding frequency. Capone, who had been surly for days in his jail cell, made no attempt to cover the scar on his face but strutted forward toward the photographers.

"Jeez," he said, a proud note in his voice, "you'd think Mussolini was passin' through."

Forcing a path through the photographers, I ushered Capone into the second car in line, Morici trailing along timidly at the end of the handcuffs like a reluctant poodle. It was just after ten-thirty when the gates swung open and we led the way out. A crowd of more than three hundred people had gathered around the gates, craning to get a glimpse of Capone.

"Keep your eyes open," I told Seager and Lahart. "You never can be certain what these monkeys will try."

After all, I remembered, one of Capone's bodyguards had actually carried a gun into federal court during the boss gangster's trial. It was a rash gesture that netted a jail term for the culprit, one Phillip D'Andrea; yet it demonstrated clearly the lengths to which the Capone hoodlums would go.

But our progress was uneventful as we drove out California Boulevard to Ogden Avenue, onto Jackson Boulevard and on over to Clark Street.

Shortly thereafter we pulled up in front of the Dearborn Station. Again there was a large group of photographers and another huge crowd of curiosity seekers. We were out of our car and beside the one bearing Capone when the doors opened. We surveyed the crowd and then, as Capone and Morici stepped to the pavement, Seager, Lahart and I began to force a path through the mob.

Cameramen protested as we battered our way through their unyielding ranks, and a camera crashed to the ground as it was struck by a shoulder in our urgent flying wedge. Morici stumbled and fell a pace behind Capone, blinking in the glare of the flashbulbs. Over the confusion I could hear Capone's exasperated bark as he tugged impatiently on the handcuffs which bound him to Morici.

"Damn it, come on," Capone snapped. "Let's get the hell out of this."

In the crowd were many of his friends. There were also his two younger brothers to greet him and say their farewells with the language of the eyes. But nobody lifted a finger to impede our progress as we crashed through the mob and passed through the gates.

There were eight cars on the Dixie Flyer this night. The one Capone was to board was second from the end. We checked the various compartments thoroughly. All of them were empty. The prisoners were then brought in and settled in one compartment with the United States marshals. The compartments on either side were occupied by guards assigned for the trip.

When I checked Capone the last time he had already stripped off his topcoat and settled down with a large cigar burning smoothly. His glance caught me as he looked up and I felt that his words were aimed directly at me.

"Well, I'm on my way to do eleven years. I've got to do it, that's all. I'm not sore at anybody."

Those hard eyes stared straight into mine.

"Some people are lucky. I wasn't."

We certainly had been, I thought, as he continued:

"There was too much overhead in my business anyhow, paying off all the time and replacing trucks and breweries. They ought to make it legitimate."

The Untouchables

I shook my head slowly.

"That's a strange idea coming from you. If it was legitimate, you certainly wouldn't want anything to do with it."

He was still watching me as I backed out into the corridor, seeing him for the last time.

My entire crew paced the wooden platform on guard duty and then watched silently as the doors of the train clanged shut and the wheels began to turn, slowly at first, for the trip which was to take Al Capone to the grim prison in the South.

We stood there, none of us saying a word, until the red lights on the tail end winked out in the distance. I didn't know what the others were thinking, but a thousand thoughts crowded through my mind.

There goes two and a half years of my life, I told myself as I stared down the tracks. It had been just about that long since the October day in 1929 when I gathered these men of mine together and told them that we were going to do the impossible and "get" Al Capone.

Well, we had done it. And the months it consumed flashed before my eyes: the killer in the candy-striped shirt, the pulse-pounding raids and wire taps, Basile's white-toothed smile that I would see no more, the defiant parade of the trucks and the killer with the dumdum bullets meant for me.

Unconsciously, my fingers had strayed to my pocket and were toying with the deadly little souvenir I kept as a good luck piece. The others had been fired on the target range. This one, with the deep cross gashed on its nose, was the only one left with my "name" on it.

"Well," Seager's deep voice shattered the stillness, "that's that. What now, I wonder?"

I thought I detected a note of relief in his voice. Why not? I know that I felt as if a terrific weight had been lifted from my shoulders now that the shadow of "Scarface Al" no longer hovered over Chicago—and over us. We had been lucky men to come through all in one piece.

What now, indeed? I didn't know. There would always be plenty of work out there in the Chicago streets for men daring enough to face it and nerves strong enough to stand it. Still on the loose were such public enemies as Klondike O'Donnell, Machine Gun Jack McGurn, Bugs Moran, Bomber Belcastro, Tough Tony Capezio and the terrible Touhys.

Yet those who remained were only muscle hoodlums, certain to be exterminated in their own feuds or by the revolver of the newest rookie patrolman. None possessed the genius for organization which had made Al Capone criminal czar of a captive city. The other men of violence would try, I thought as we walked out into the night, but they would be conquered by the workaday channels of the law.

Only then did it come to me that the work of "The Untouchables" was ended.

EPILOGUE

With the conclusion of the Capone case, "The Untouchables" were disbanded and Ness, in recognition of his work,
was named Chief Investigator of Prohibition Forces in the
entire Chicago division.

The following year, 1933, the F.B.I. moved him to Cin-
cinnati with instructions to clean up the dangerous "Moon-
shine Mountains" of Kentucky, Tennessee and Ohio. For two
years he was a "revenooer" and narrowly missed being shot
from ambush a number of times as he confiscated hundreds
of hillbilly stills.

"Those mountain men and their squirrel rifles gave me
almost as many chills as the Capone mob," he admitted.

Next came assignment to the Northern District of Ohio as
investigator in charge of the Treasury Department's Alcoholic Tax Unit, with offices in Cleveland. When that city
elected a reform ticket in 1935, Ness, because of his reputation, was approached to direct an investigation of police
department corruption. Becoming the city's youngest Direc-

tor of Public Safety, a post he held for six years, he forced two hundred resignations and sent a dozen high officers to the state prison.

During those years, Ness established the Cleveland Police Academy, reorganized the traffic bureau and founded a Cleveland Boys' Town. These feats earned him the Veteran of Foreign Wars medal as Cuyahoga County's outstanding citizen.

With the advent of World War II, Ness served from 1941 though 1945 as Director of Social Protection for the Federal Security Agency, combating venereal disease in and near every military establishment in the United States. For this work he received the Navy's Meritorious Service Citation in 1946.

It was only after World War II that Ness finally utilized his college training and entered the business world. With his wife—the former Betty Andersen—and their eleven-year-old son, Bobby, he moved to Coudersport, Pennsylvania, where he became president of the Guaranty Paper Corporation and Fidelity Check Corporation.

Preparation of "The Untouchables" was one of his chief interests for more than two years. But Eliot Ness did not see the finished product. On May 16, 1957, shortly after approving the final galleys, he died suddenly of a heart attack.

This is his memorial, as well as that of "The Untouchables."

OSCAR FRALEY